NIGHT, AGAIN

NIGHT, AGAIN

Contemporary
fiction from
VIETNAM

Edited by
LINH DINH

SEVEN STORIES PRESS
New York • Toronto • London • Melbourne

Seven Stories Press
140 Watts Street
New York, NY 10013
http://www.sevenstories.com/

In Canada:
Publishers Group Canada, 250A Carlton Street, Toronto, ON M5A 2L1

In the U.K.:
Turnaround Publisher Services Ltd., Unit 3, Olympia Trading Estate,
Coburg Road, Wood Green, London N22 6TZ

In Australia:
Palgrave Macmillan, 627 Chapel Street, South Yarra, VIC 3141

College professors may order examination copies of Seven Stories Press
titles for a free six-month trial period. To order, visit www.sevenstories.com/
textbook/ or send a fax on school letterhead to 212-226-1411.

Library of Congress Cataloging-in-Publication Data
Dinh, Linh, 1963–
  Night, again : contemporary fiction from Vietnam / edited by Linh
Dinh.— 2nd ed.
      p. cm.
  Includes bibliographical references.
  ISBN-13: 978-1-58322-706-0 (pbk. : alk. paper)
  ISBN-10: 1-58322-706-7 (pbk. : alk. paper)
  1. Short stories, Vietnamese—20th century—Translations into English.
I. Title.

PL4378.82.E5D46 2006
895.9'2230108034—dc22

                                                    2006002286

Printed in the USA

9 8 7 6 5 4 3 2 1

CONTENTS

ACKNOWLEDGMENTS

*F*or their encouragement and advice, I wish to thank Hoang Ngoc Hien, Truong Vu, Peter Zinoman, Nguyen Nguyet Cam, Dan Duffy, and Nguyen Qui Duc. Without their considerable expertise, this volume would not have been possible. I also wish to thank Dan Simon of Seven Stories, who initiated this project and supported it through to completion; to Cynthia Cameros and Elinor Nauen, for their sensitive proofreading of the text; to sculptor Van Thuyet, who shuttled me to various meetings around Hanoi; and to the following individuals, who graciously provided me with timely favors: Le Minh Khue, David Deifer, Bob Malloy, Phong Bui, Rosemary Kacorocski, Amanda Zinoman, Jason Zinoman, Mai Nguyen, Mitch Epstein, Susan Bell, Vinh Nguyen, Allen Reidy, and Pat Matsueda.

INTRODUCTION

Argue with a smart man,
Can't win.
Argue with a stupid man,
Can't stop.

—Vietnamese proverb

I

𝒯he role of literature as moral beacon
has deep roots in Vietnam. In pre-modern times, court mandarins were those who had passed an examination on the Chinese classics. Almost always, the poet was also a public servant. The Confucian dictum "literate men show the way" meant literature's role was to steer the masses toward righteousness. Writing that is irreverent, playful, or morally ambivalent—as in that of Nguyen Du, Ho Xuan Huong, and much of the oral tradition—was seen by the ruling class as either frivolous or subversive. Since the majority of people was illiterate, with no access to either Chinese or the native "Nom" script, the written word was also imbued with a solemn, quasi-mystical air, further reinforcing its stature as a moral guide.

With the twentieth century came the adoption of the romanized script, the rise of general literacy, and the propagation of middle- and lowbrow cultures. Prose fiction made its appearance for the first time. Unlike lyrical poetry, which has a long heritage, narratives had existed solely in verse (the supreme example of Vietnamese verse narrative is Nguyen Du's "The Tale of Kieu," a 3,254 line poem composed in

1814).[1] The only pre-modern examples of Vietnamese prose narratives were a handful of collections of fantastic tales, often derived from folklore, such as the fourteenth-century *Viet Dien U Linh Tap* [*Supernatural Tales from the Viet Realm*] or the fifteenth-century *Linh Nam Chich Quai* [*Weird Stories from the South*]. Transcribing folktales is not the same as writing fiction; hence, conscious, deliberate composition in prose did not appear in Vietnam until the beginning of the twentieth century.

French and Chinese novels in translation provided creative models for the earliest Vietnamese fiction writers. During the first two decades of this century, the prolific Nguyen Van Vinh translated Dumas' *Les Trois Mousequetaires*, Hugo's *Les Misérables*, and Balzac's *La Peau de Chagrin*, among others, while the critic Pham Quynh was responsible for Vietnamese versions of stories by Maupassant, Pierre Loti, and Alfred de Vigny. Two of the earliest novels, *Ai Lam Duoc?* [*Who Can Do It?*] (1912) by Ho Bieu Chanh and *To Tam* [*Pure Heart*] (1925) by Hoang Ngoc Phach, were modeled after *Andre Cornelis* by Paul Bourget and *La Dame aux Camelias* by Alexander Dumas, fils, respectively. Phan Duy Ton, a pioneer writer, apprenticed himself by tapping into the vernacular and published, under a pseudonym, a two-volume collection of bawdy anecdotes, *Tieu Lam Annam* [*Annamese Humor*] in 1922. Many writers shunted their mother tongue to compose in French, the language they were taught in the lycees. To those who chose this option, the critic Pham Quynh warned: "In borrowing someone's language, you are also borrowing his ideas, literary techniques—even his emotions and customs." [2] After centuries of writing in Chinese, the Vietnamese had produced no Li Po, Quynh pointed out, and writing in French, it is unlikely that they will ever produce a Victor Hugo or an Anatole France.[3] After reading a story in French, the critic suggested, as an exercise, to try retelling it to one's wife in Vietnamese.[4]

From this beginning, Vietnamese fiction matured quickly through the 1930s, a relatively stable period politically, producing writers—Vu Trong Phung, for example—of enduring interest. But the onset of war and revolution, from the late '30s onward, brought the intrusion of dogma into the life of the imagination. In a 1951 letter addressed to artists, Ho Chi Minh declared: "To fulfill his task, the cultural fighter needs a firm point of view and correct ideas. . . . [T]he goods of the resistance, the country, and the people must be considered above all else." [5]

II

With the exception of the mid- and late-'80s, which ushered in a period of liberalization known as *Doi Moi,* writers in Socialist Vietnam could be harassed under the most bizarre pretexts. In 1956, the poet Tran Dan was arrested for capitalizing "Man" in a brief passage of a rambling poem cataloging social despair, since such a designation was reserved for Ho Chi Minh.[6] Even in 1991, Le Minh Khue could still be criticized for having a fictional female NVA soldier be mesmerized by a smile from a handsome South Vietnamese prisoner of war.[7] To fall in love with the enemy is an ideological no-no—a violation of the tenets of Socialist Realism, which bifurcates the world into progressive and reactionary, with all moral and even physical flaws prescribed for members of the latter. In such a climate, the North produced almost no literature of artistic worth from 1954 until 1975.

After unification, the literature of the South, which was branded as an offshoot of U.S. neocolonialism, was snuffed out through confiscation, burning of books, and arrest of authors. By 1978, three years after the fall of Saigon, there were 163 confirmed cases of writers formerly active in the South detained in reeducation camps. In his memoir *Dai Hoc Mau,*[8] Pham Vinh Xuan recounted an interrogation session that mixes terror with farce. Arrested as an ARVN officer, Xuan concealed the fact that he wrote under the pseudonym Ha

Thuc Sinh. After being whacked a few times with an aluminum stick, he admitted to his literary activities. Based on the "evidence" that he had published ten books, his captors then accused him of working for either the CIA or a phantom CIB. Xuan recounted in his memoir:

> "I was a soldier in charge of logistics at the naval center. I had nothing to do with the CIA."
>
> The security guy lifted the stick, changed his mind suddenly, then screamed: "You are one stubborn bastard, always denying everything. . . . I'll tell you the truth: A military officer like you who wrote reactionary books on the side had to be employed by either the CIA or the CIB." [9]

III

The upheavals in the Communist world in the mid-'80s had profound repercussions in Vietnam. After the 1986 Party congress, the term *Doi Moi*—or "Renovation," the Vietnamese version of glasnost—entered the vernacular. In literature, the new era was announced by Secretary General Nguyen Van Linh at a gathering of writers in October of 1987. Admitting that the Party had been "less than democratic [in the past], and often dogmatic and brutal" in its treatment of writers, Linh promised to "unbind" them from that point on: "Speak the truth. . . . No matter what happens, Comrades, don't curb your pen." [10]

The Party was only conceding what was already happening. The Doi Moi literature can be traced to the appearances of novels by Ma Van Khang, Le Luu, and Duong Thu Huong in 1985, 1986, and 1987, respectively, with essays by the prominent critic Hoang Ngoc Hien and the writer-critic Nguyen Minh Chau serving as catalysts. All had impeccable political pedigrees: Khang, Luu, Huong, and Chau were Party members who had served in the war (Chau retired as a colonel); Hien is the director of the Nguyen Du writing school, originally modeled after the Gorky school in Moscow, established to develop Socialist writers.

Although the situation has been volatile, with books still being banned, editors fired, and authors silenced, the government's tactics are not nearly as draconian as in the past. In 1958, Nguyen Dang, Thuy An, and Tran Hieu Thao had been slapped with 15-year sentences in kangaroo courts for their involvement in the Nhan Van Giai Pham movement.[11]

IV

The wide circulation of Duong Thu Huong's first novel, *Ben Kia Bo Ao Vong* [*The Other Side of Illusion*] (1987), established her in the vanguard of *Doi Moi* literature. Though her roots are in Socialist Realism, Huong has broken from the movement's sanctioned subjects by listing Party members among her targets of criticism. Later, with the appearance of *Nhung Thien Duong Mu* [*Paradise of the Blind*] (1988) and *Tieu Thuyet Vo De* [*Novel Without a Name*] (1994) in foreign translations, plus her increasing outspokenness and a seven-month imprisonment in 1991, Huong became Vietnam's most visible writer and dissident. Politics notwithstanding, her gift as a writer is as a purveyor of the quotidian. In the words of one critic: "She is unmatched in her ability to capture the small, telling details of everyday life." [12]

Huong's first book, a volume of stories called *Chan Dung Nguoi Hang Xom* [*Portrait of a Neighbor*] (1985), reveals both her strengths and weaknesses. In the story "Tho Lam Mong Tay" ["The Nail Technician"], fine descriptive passages are perverted by a heavy-handed political subtext. Its bias can be traced to the war, in which both North and South had demonized each other:

> Two cousins, separated for 21 years by the civil war, met again when the narrator, a member of the victorious army, arrived in Saigon in 1975. She found Sang, once "a fit, alert child, with a ruddy

complexion," who had vowed to take revenge on the
French for killing his father, turned into a pale, listless man obsequiously painting women's toenails.
Sang lived with a busty wife in "a sort of hovel" next
to an open sewer, where they bickered endlessly. As
a mascot for the decadent South, Sang's two solaces
were his electric guitar and prostitutes. A circus act
in the zoo, featuring a midget with two monkeys,
provided the narrator with an apt analogy to ram
the author's point home: "Out there [in the North],
we do not debase ourselves like that, no matter how
much money we can make."

A story in the same volume, "Hoi Quang Cua Mua Xuan"
["Reflections of Spring"], included in this anthology, show-
cases Huong's literary gifts sans soapbox. As her vision
matured, Huong's technique transformed seamlessly from
Socialist Realism to Social Realism. Other authors—most
notably the acerbic, funny and occasionally misanthropic Le
Minh Khue—join her as writers of conscience in debunking
the Socialist utopia. In place of what the historian Peter
Zinoman termed "a canned cheeriness . . . central to the
'morality building' function of the revolutionary writers" [13]
are bleak portraits of a backward, rundown and corrupt society. Indignant and with an agenda, their goals are not the
same as those who, while not eschewing polemics alto-
gether, busy themselves with words and the intangibles of
living.

V

Unfettered by the exigencies of war and politics, many writers
are plumbing their own subjectivity and reinventing the multi-
faceted self. No "cultural fighters," the only vindication they
need is to write well. Pham Thi Hoai declared: "When a writer
publishes a good piece of work, he is contributing to changing
society. His intention is not to lunge noisily forward to change

society, but if the piece is good, one way or another it has already served its social function." [14] In the works of Hoai, Do Phuoc Tien, Nguyen Huy Thiep, among others, complex events and emotions are rendered in language both suggestive and opaque. Totalitarian, dogmatic truth is replaced by playful indeterminacy. In one story of Thiep's, the reader is offered a choice of three endings. In an addendum to another, a scholar friend of the narrator refutes the story proper with a photograph, and hectors the narrator/author to stick to the "principles of realism." In many of Pham Thi Hoai's stories, unusual phrasings and diction expose language as mere artifice.

Educated at the University of Humbolt and a translator of Kafka, Hoai, a major player in *Doi Moi* literature, now lives in Berlin. It is interesting to note how many other important writers have emigrated or spent significant time overseas. Duong Thu Huong lived in Russia, and the protagonist of her most successful novel, *Nhung Thien Duong Mu* [*Paradise of the Blind*], is a Vietnamese "guest worker" in the former Soviet Union. The gifted and highly touted Tran Vu escaped Vietnam by boat at the age of sixteen and was raised in France. Published in California, Vu's fiction, populated mostly by Vietnamese characters living inside or outside of Vietnam, alternates between a crisp, no-nonsense prose and a perversely wrought archaism, extending the language in contrary directions.

Although it may be invigorated by foreign influences, the soul of any literature lies in its relationship to the vernacular. Often overlooked in the buzz surrounding Nguyen Huy Thiep—Vietnam's most influential writer—is his exceptional ear for the language. Thiep's sophisticated yet earthy fiction is enlivened by many memorable phrases culled from ordinary speech. A teacher in remote Son La province for ten years, he now runs a restaurant in Hanoi, a stone's throw from a much-bombed bridge on the Red River. At forty-five, he has never traveled abroad. Considering the paucity of translated books in Vietnam, even since the easing of state censorship, Thiep's eclectic reading list, as revealed in his own essays and interviews, is an index to the mental life of a contemporary Hanoi intellectual: all the great Vietnamese poets, from the fifteenth-century Nguyen Trai to Nguyen Du; Chinese modern fiction pioneer Lu Tsun; first-century B.C. Chinese historian Si Ma Quan (in Phan Ngoc's translation); *The Three Kingdoms*; Dostoyevsky, Gogol, Gorky, Maupassant, Camus, Goethe, Tagore, Neruda, the Bible. Western and overseas Vietnamese critics, in assessing his varied output, have tripped over each other to point out his affinities with experimental writers such as Borges, Eco, and Rushdie, most of whom he has never heard of. Like Europeans discovering Modernism through African sculptures, Thiep arrived at something like Post-Modernism through the goblin stories of *Linh Nam Chich Quai* and the lore of the Black Thai minority.[15]

The stories in *Night, Again* testify to the resilience of literature in a country which does not reward and often punishes its best writers, where the most famous author, Huong, is banned, and the most accomplished is an erudite maitre d'. For those in exile, there is an unreality of writing in a language one does not hear everyday, for a tiny and scattered audience. Still, the need to probe one's experiences through fiction persist stubbornly, in spite of the question: "Dear monkey, who needs a talented writer?" [16]

Linh Dinh
Philadelphia
January 1996

NOTES

1. Available in English in Huynh Sanh Thong's translation, *The Tale of Kieu* (New Haven: Yale University Press, 1987).
2. Pham Quynh, "Quoc Hoc Voi Quoc Van." *Nam Phong* 164, July 1931.
3. Pham Quynh, "Ban Ve Quoc Hoc." *Nam Phong* 163, June 1931.
4. Pham Quynh, "Van Quoc Ngu." Thuong Chi Van Tap I. (Saigon: Bo Quoc Gia Giao Duc, 1962), p. 49.
5. Quoted in Nguyen Hung Quoc's *Van Hoc Vietnam Duoi Che Do Cong San* (Westminster: Van Nghe, 1991), p. 17.
6. Hoang Van Chi, *Tram Hoa Dua No Tren Dat Bac* (Saigon: Mat Tran Tu Do Bao Ve Van Hoa, 1959).
7. Le Minh Khue, "Mong Manh Nhu La Tia Nang," in the collection *Truyen Ngan* (Hanoi: Nha Xuat Ban Van Hoc, 1994).
8. Ha Thuc Sinh. *Dai Hoc Mau.* (San Jose: Nhan Van, 1985). "Dai Hoc Mau" is an original pun meaning both "Blood University" and "spitting out blood."
9. Ibid, p. 131.
10. Nguyen Hung Quoc, op. cit., p. 343.
11. *Nhan Van Giai Pham* was the name of a dissident literary movement that lasted between 1956 and 1958 in North Vietnam. *Nhan Van* was the name of a literary journal in Vietnam and *Giai Pham* translates as "beautiful objects." The name of the movement is, thus, "*Nhan Van's* Beautiful Objects."
12. Hue-Tam Ho Tai, "Duong Thu Huong and the Literature of Disenchantment," *Vietnam Forum*, no. 14, 1994.
13. Peter Zinoman, "Declassifying Nguyen Huy Thiep," *Positions*, 2:2, Fall 1994.
14. Filmed interview with Amanda Zinoman, Peter Zinoman and Nguyen Nguyet Cam, Hanoi, 1992.
15. See Peter Zinoman's excellent essay, "Declassifying Nguyen Huy Thiep," op. cit.
16. Nguyen Huy Thiep addressing himself, in his essay "Mot Goc So Xuat Trong The Gioi Noi Tam Nha Van," *Hop Luu*, no. 1, October, 1991.

SLEEPING ON EARTH

Nguyen Thi Am

*I*t was in the back streets, near the train stations, that the homeless gathered. They earned their living there, honestly, dishonestly. Honestly, as dockers, carriers of buckets of water and *cyclo* drivers. The dishonest professions are too numerous to mention. The homeless like to gamble. The men played *ba cay* and *to tom* or rolled dice. For the women, it was cards. The dreams born from those games crushed the ones that life had to offer them. They weren't wrong.

Wherever they live, human beings are human beings. God, in creating them, gave them the same right to love. So dirty kids accompanied the wandering of the homeless.

One evening, in a deserted alley near the bus station, three middle-aged women in rags were playing cards.

"A pair of black pawns," said the fat one, chuckling, and showed her hand.

"What bad luck," sighed the skinniest one.

"It's your own fault. You should have played it safe," grumbled the third, whose face was pockmarked.

The losers fished money out of the hem of their pants and paid up, grumbling. Next to them lay a half-naked baby in a ragged shirt. He must have been a year old. He was sleeping.

The quarrel between the players woke him up, and he howled. He was no angel. Between his little thighs, black with filth, nestled a tiny penis the size of a plum. Furious, the little penis shot a stream of urine in an arch. His bawling bothered the players.

The fat one said, "Calm the kid down. He's gonna burst our eardrums."

"Who cares," said the woman with the pockmarked face.

The baby, abandoned, cried even louder. The game was interrupted. The pockmarked woman looked over at the kid, furious. The little boy was purple with rage. Screaming like that—you would have thought it was an ambulance siren. The pockmarked woman had just lost. She stretched out a thin, filthy hand with long, flamboyant nails painted the scarlet color of ten-o'clock flowers. Gritting her teeth, she slapped the baby's bottom.

The little one really let loose then. Exasperated, the two women looked over at the pockmarked woman.

"Rent him out. If he keeps screaming like that, we're going to have to stop the game."

That's what the fat one said. The pockmarked woman turned around:

"Hey, Thuy, come over here, I'll rent him to you . . ."

She gestured with her hand. Nearby, shadows swarmed around the dented pots and pans. A twenty-year-old girl pulled herself out and approached, dragging her feet. A hat made out of bamboo leaves covered her head. She took the baby and said: "You got any Seduxen left, Elder Sister?"

"Here." The pockmarked woman pulled a half-opened packet of sleeping pills and handed it to the girl. The girl took a pill and returned the packet. The little one was still screaming. She picked it up and brought it over to the public fountain. The fountain hissed softly, dripping slowly, drop by drop. Too slowly. The girl pulled open the kid's jaw violently and dropped the pill in. She scooped up water from the puddle under the spout in her hand and poured it into his mouth. The baby swallowed the pill, choking. And she carried him away.

The woman with the pockmarked face, for a time deeply absorbed in her card game, looked up now. She shouted after the girl:

"Hey! That's going to be 5,000 *dong*. Don't forget to give him a bowl of rice gruel when he wakes up!" The girl didn't respond. She trudged off toward the town.

"A pair of black horses!" shrieked the woman with the pockmarked face, giving her thigh a slap. Astounded, the two other women paid up.

The baby fell into a drugged sleep, slumping over the young girl's arm like a wet towel. Evening fell. A young peasant in rags with a baby in her arms: nothing like it if you want to move the hearts of men.

The wind blew in from the North. The amber light of the sun had disappeared. Above, two black clouds banked in the sky. The rain fell in a drizzle. Then drops spattered the pavement of the road. The young girl carried the baby through the rain. Her conical hat protected her head and her breast. Further down, her body, and the baby's thighs, streamed with rain. People who had taken shelter on the sidewalk called to her, worried. She went her own way. The rain wove a weft for all of life's dramas. She too needed this . . .

Hanoi train station. The electronic clock read quarter to six. The nightlife was just beginning. Every day tens of thousands of human beings passed through here. Hundreds of them had yet to encounter the drama of their day. The young girl wove through the waiting passengers. She cried as she walked. Her tears flowed, slowly, silently. From time to time, she would stop in the middle of the crowd. An old man turned away, unable to bear the sight of her. A few well-dressed city dwellers smiled knowingly. She didn't bother holding out her hand to them. City dwellers live in their civility. They didn't belong to her world. They might denounce her act. In spite of everything, armed as she was, she still had hope.

A mature man, graying at the temples, in uniform, looked over in her direction, bothered. He asked her: "Why don't you change clothes? You're going to catch cold."

"Yes. The harvest was bad. We have nothing left to eat. We're trying to survive by begging."

"Where's your husband?"

"He sacrificed himself in Cambodia."

"And your family?"

"It's not worth talking about . . ."

She wept. The man, embarrassed, thought a moment.

"Here, I'll give you a bit of money. Go buy some dry clothes for the baby. Give him something to eat or he's going to come down with pneumonia."

He opened his leather bag and got out a wad of bills. He took half of them, handing the girl 20,000 *dong*. The girl wiped away her tears and took the money.

"Thank you."

And she left. The man lit a cigarette. He felt gripped by a strange sadness. The girl was about the same age as his eldest daughter.

Five minutes later, in the waiting room, an old farmer, who looked rich, gave the girl 5,000 *dong*.

An hour later, at the entrance to the train station, two young soldiers gave her another 5,000 *dong*.

It was an uncertain evening, the rain falling intermittently. Two young prostitutes wandered in vain inside the station. Jealous, they smoked and bitched. "What a dog's life! That little peasant is making a fortune!"

"I've been watching her from the beginning of the evening. She must have brought in more than 100,000 *dong*."

"From now until dawn she'll probably bring it to 200,000."

The rain fell again. Time goes fast when you're involved in what you're doing. The train station clock started to sing. The two hands pointed at midnight. It was over. The young girl jumped up and hurried back. The kid woke up. This time, he was weak with hunger, exhausted by the sleeping pill. He stared up at the girl, wide-eyed. She thought of taking him to a rice stall. But she was afraid of being late. The woman with the pockmarked face would certainly demand a late fee if she took time to feed the baby.

She walked back through deserted streets. Under a wide roof, two bodies were asleep under raincoats. She nudged them with her foot. A raincoat moved. The woman with the pockmarked face poked her head out from under the covers. "Where's the money? . . . Why are you bringing him back so late?"

The girl held out a 5,000-*dong* bill.

"Did you give him something to eat?"

"Yeah. It's done."

The little one looked up at his mother. A vacant look, neither sad nor happy. A man lay next to her. The face of a hired killer. He grumbled, angry at having been wakened. The woman with the pockmarked face took the baby under her arm. She placed it between the two of them. The kid fell asleep between his mother and the man.

The young girl left. The man and the woman pulled their raincoats over their heads and fell back asleep.

And time passed. One hour . . . Two hours . . . Three hours . . . Five hours. The sky grew lighter. The woman with the pockmarked face shifted about for a moment under her raincoat, and then woke up. She lifted the baby. His body was blackish. He was dead. A mother always suffers from the loss of a child. She let out the cries of a mad dog. One human being . . . Two human beings . . . Three human beings . . . People crowded around to see the unusual incident. Two policemen approached, curious. They dispersed the crowd. They called a *cyclo* and ordered him to drive the mother and the child to the hospital.

Souls who have suffered down here on earth go to heaven. When he arrived, the little one told his friends: "During my stay on earth, all I did was sleep. Life down there is just one long sleep."

Translated by Phan Huy Duong and Nina McPherson

A MARKER ON THE SIDE OF THE BOAT *

Bao Ninh

*O*n my life, I've been here, there, but I've had few chances to visit Hanoi. Once when I was little, once during the war, and a couple times years later. That's why, aside from Turtle Lake and Long Bien Bridge, I can only recall Hang Co Train Station and a street with trolley tracks on it. But in spite of this, when I shut my eyes to peer into the crevices of my memory, I can always conjure up, if only dimly, a general image of its streets. This remote, alien city, with which I have had no intimacy, had, over the years, silently insinuated itself into my consciousness as a beloved place. It is a love born out of nothing, less of an emotion than a light sensation, melancholic, plotless, a souvenir from my war-filled youth, a youth that although long-gone, still reverberates with its echoes. Like the sounds of rain, of wind blowing through a room or of leaves falling, never to be forgotten.

Twenty years have already passed. Hanoi back then and Hanoi today must be as different as sky and earth.

That day, I was driving my division commander from the battle of Quang Tri to a meeting at military headquarters, outside the capital. We arrived to find the city in a state of siege. It was truly a life-and-death battle, a blood struggle which,

---

* The title refers to a folktale about a fisherman who, to mark the spot where he dropped his sword into a lake, made a mark on the side of his boat.

after twelve days and nights, would change the faces of both winner and loser. In such a dire situation, I did not dare request a leave to visit my village; I only asked for permission to go into the city to deliver a handful of letters given to me by my buddies who were from Hanoi. I wanted to visit each family so I could receive a letter in turn, to bring a little joy back to our soldiers. On Christmas day, I was given permission to go into town, and was told to be back by midnight.

Without knowing the neighborhoods, and with nine letters to deliver, I still wasn't worried. I thought I would find the first address, then ask for directions to go to the next one. I didn't anticipate having to slip each one of those letters under the door. That day, all of Hanoi seemed to have been abandoned.

By the time I had delivered my last letter, the sky was pitch-dark. The long, deserted street lay soaked in rain, punctuated by dim circles of streetlights. I asked for direction to Vong. A militiaman in a frond jacket kindly escorted me for a stretch. At a three-way intersection, before we parted, he pointed to the trolley tracks hugging the sidewalk and said to follow them to get to my destination.

With my helmet on and my collar up, I plunged into that fine gauze of drizzle. The night was chilly. The tracks were like a trail forging through the jungle of darkened houses. A city during wartime, on a precipice, abandoned. I walked on doggedly, my body numbed. There were endless dark stretches without a single pedestrian or a stall. The night exhaled its cold, wet air, soaking me right down to my empty stomach. My joints felt stiff, aching, as if ready to be jarred apart. A fever that had been simmering all evening crept up my spine. I couldn't stop shivering. My brain slowed down. My knees felt like buckling. I hadn't even walked that far, and already I was counting my steps. Without seeing where I was going, I almost ran into the front of a trolley, a black mass parked in the middle of the street.

I staggered onto the sidewalk and wobbled beneath the eaves of a house. With my back leaning against the door, teeth chattering, I slowly slid down until I was sitting on the wet step, cold as a block of ice. My heart was freezing. I groaned until I could groan no more. My shivering became more violent. My body temperature was at a dangerous level. I thought numbly:

"If I'm not careful this could be the end. Other people stricken with fever die on a hammock in the middle of a jungle. I'll die sitting up, certainly, to be metamorphosed into a rock in front of someone's door."

Above my head, the corrugated tin roof shivered. The wind blew the rain right onto the stoop. Already wet, I got wetter. Dizzy, breathing in gulps, I knew I had to marshal all my energy to get up and continue, but I had no willpower left. It was draining out of me like water from a broken vase. At that point, the door behind me inched open. I heard the noise but could make no sense of it. Unconsciousness, like a letting-go and a sigh of relief, seduced me from my own body . . .

Time stopped for I don't know how long. I opened my eyes slowly. My consciousness settled on a rim of light. Still wobbly, uncertain, I nevertheless knew I was indoors, and no longer delirious. The walls appeared to have been painted a pale green, although faded with time. The ceiling was dark. The warm air redolent of camphor. I shifted lightly. The bed creaked beneath my body. I was under a blanket, with my head on a pillow: tranquil, dried, warm, it was unreal. I turned my body. On a night table by the corner of the room, a small oil lamp gave off a dirty yellow light. A clock kept time by monotonously ticking off the seconds. The sudden thought of time startled me; I groaned.

"Oh, Brother . . ." Someone's hand caressed my cheek, and a soft, soothing voice whispered, "You've recovered. I was really worried . . ."

My heart froze, then beat wildly. I was embarrassed. What was happening; who was this woman?

"I . . ." I finally opened my mouth, tongue-tied, stuttering, "Where am I . . . Where is this?"

"This is my house, Brother." Her soft hand touched my forehead. "You are my guest."

I tried to regain my composure, my strength. Breathing

deeply, I turned toward my hostess. She was sitting on the edge of the bed, with her face beyond the lamp's illumination. I could only make out her shoulders and her hair.

"You still have a touch of that fever, Brother, but you've gotten much better, luckily. You scared the hell out of me in the beginning. I was frightened to death."

"I'm in trouble . . ." I gasped, "It's past time for me to report back. I, I have to go . . ."

"Oh, Brother, you're in no shape to go anywhere. Outside, in the cold, you'll only get sick again. Besides, your clothes are being hung to dry in the kitchen. You can't wear them yet. They're still damp."

What? I realized what had happened. I quickly touched my thigh and chest, shuddering, wishing I could contract my body. Beneath the quilted blanket, I was practically naked. "I'll bring you some rice gruel from the kitchen, all right?" The woman spoke casually and got up from the bed. "There is a change of clothing by the pillow for you to wear. It's also an army uniform."

Without taking the oil lamp, she turned and walked out the door into the darkness. I threw the blanket aside and sprang out of bed. The strong aroma of medicinal balm from beneath the blanket stung my eyes. I dressed quickly. The uniform, new, reeking of camphor, was a reasonable fit. Decked out like a soldier again, I seemed to have regained my strength, although my entire body ached, my head was numb, and a ringing lingered in my ears.

As tired as I was, I could detect, immediately, the smell of hot rice gruel as it was being brought into the room by my hostess. She walked softly, her clogs barely making a noise on the wooden floor. She placed the tray on the table and turned up the knob on the oil lamp.

"The rain has stopped," she said, then sighed, for no apparent reason.

In the dimness of that room, I stared silently. This wonderful stranger was like an illusion conjured up in front of my eyes. An unearthly illusion, kind and beautiful. Kind and beautiful, her face, her eyes and lips, although I never really had a chance to look at her. The moment had arrived for this city. Within a fraction of a second, there won't be time for heaven and earth to react, no time to even shudder.

Something monstrous, violent, suddenly stabbed the silence. Out of nowhere, a reconnaissance plane—just one—thunderously slashed its way across the sky, skimming the city's rooftops. Inside the room, even the oil lamp seemed to be holding its breath . . .

"I think it's gone," she whispered, trembling, a pale smile on her face. "They're just trying to scare us."

"Yes," I said, "Only some spy trying to sneak up on us, don't . . ."

I was trying to reassure her, to tell her there was nothing to be scared of, when the horrible air siren started wailing, interrupting my sentence. Although I had heard it many times in previous nights and had learned to anticipate the sound, the air siren still made my heart freeze. Never before had this messenger of death reverberated so terrifyingly. The way it howled and screamed—desperate, angry, hysterical—made people want to scream along with it. "B-52s, B-52s, B-52s are coming!" the public speaker frantically blared. "B-52s! Ninety kilometers from Hanoi. Eighty kilometers."

"Those Americans!" I said. "They're coming. That last guy was a scout."

"Yes. It's the B-52s. One more night."

"We'll have to go to the shelter!" I couldn't hide my nervousness. "They're getting near. Quick!"

"But how are you feeling?" She sighed, filled with childish concern. "It's very cold outside."

My premonition of danger suddenly became more palpable. With my mouth dry, my throat contracted, the drum in my chest was banging away. Never before had my intuition deceived me.

"Eat some, Brother, while it's still hot . . ."

"No!" I said, my voice hoarse, "Hot cold nothing! The bombs are falling soon. They're carpet-bombing us!"

"How do you know?" she blurted in terror.

"I can smell it! Quick! To the shelter!" I practically shouted.

After blowing out the lamp, she grabbed me by the wrist and led me out of the room. My tenseness had been transferred to her. Gasping, her clogs beat a fierce rhythm on the floor. We went down the stairs, then had to pass through a long, narrow, wet corridor before making it to the street. The rain had stopped. The sky had cleared up somewhat. The air was crisp, transparent, eerie. In the middle of the street, right outside the door, the same trolley sullenly sat, like a stranded ship.

On the sidewalk, the personal shelter, cast out of cement, gaped open its black mouth.

"We should go to the public shelter, Brother," the woman said between quick breaths, "I never want to go inside one of these round ones. There's stagnant water at the bottom. It's gross."

"Now this!" I said, irritated.

"It's only down the street, Brother. Plus, there will be lots of people. It won't be so scary."

We lunged forward into the wind. The entire city was in hiding. In the deadly silence, there were only the two of us, a couple alone in the midst of terror. The seconds ticked by but our escape route seemed endless. A three-way intersection. Then a four-way intersection. The public shelter was nowhere in sight. Wearing those clogs, she couldn't run. But then, oh God, it was already too late to run. Artillery was opening up in the outlying areas. The loud roars of 100-millimeter guns going off in unison. Brilliant flashes. Flame arrows, in pairs, thunderously lunging upward, tearing into the cloud ceiling, leaving red trails behind them. Surrounded by the frantic sounds of our troops' firepower, I could sense what was about to happen in the sky above. I had seen much carnage on the battlefield as a foot soldier. I knew how much chance there is in life-and-death matters. For the two of us, I knew it was over. The bombs were about to fall right on that street.

Fate had wickedly placed us in the middle of a long street with no houses on either side, only high walls running into the distance. By the flashes of the long-range artilleries, I could detect no personal shelters on either sidewalk. It was death's ideal coordinates. A few more hurried steps would not have made a difference.

"They're dropping them!" I said and grabbed her arm.

"Brother, only a little more!"

"We don't have time," I calmly said, with unearthly composure. "The bombs are coming right now. Lie down, quickly, and don't panic."

She obediently lay down next to me, at the foot of a brick wall. She was very confused and only half-believed my deadly pronouncements. But I knew that, within ten seconds or less, the bombs would come. The B-52s, those monstrous dragons, sowers of terror, were no strangers to me. In the South, they would fly at a lower altitude during the day, in formations of three or six planes, arrogantly across the sky, sowing streaks of thick smoke behind them as their bombs rained down. These rains could collapse a side of a mountain, bury a stretch of a river, or wipe out an entire forest. But this was no rain; the sky itself was falling. In the place of mountains and forests were houses and streets. The sky was one vast menace, and the city appeared as small as the palm of a hand. In the face of such destruction, I thought, how flimsy is human life. I tensed and waited.

It was as if I didn't hear the explosions. Although I was anticipating the noise, it still took me by surprise. My vision abruptly darkened. The earth shuddered, writhed. Space itself became distorted. Something burning, sharp, slapped me in the face. Heat from the bombs filled my lungs.

She rolled toward me, seeking shelter—her cold body pressing against mine; her breath on my stunned, sweaty face; her hair disheveled.

Another string of bombs came, this time appearing to be right on the other side of the wall. Earth, rocks, cement, roof tiles, houses, all blew up together. The heavens screamed, shattered. Waves of heat rolled across the earth's surface. Die now! Die now! Die . . . ie . . . ie. I clutched her, clenching my teeth, waiting for that split second when our bones and flesh would be torn asunder. The bombs came steadily, savagely, howling, exploding one after another.

After every explosion, every wave of heat, our bodies coiled more tightly together. The crushing shift in atmospheric pressure left us reeling, stupefied.

Suddenly, death relaxed its claws. The big door in the sky was slammed shut. Silence. The explosion of the last bomb stopped all the others.

We continued to lie still, clutching each other. It was as if we had become paralyzed, incredulous at the fact that we were still alive. We kept in that position for a long time before she wriggled herself free from my grasp.

I slowly helped her to get up. With a shoulder of her shirt torn, her hair disheveled, fear in her eyes, she groped with her feet trying to find her clogs, those useless high-heeled clogs. Billows of thick smoke drifted by. There was a burnt smell of bomb powder in the air. The sky was a bruised red.

As the humming subsided in my ears, I could hear, from somewhere nearby, voices crying for help. The whole neighborhood quickly went into a clamor. A crowd emerged, frantically rushing forward with picks, shovels, crowbars and stretchers.

"Don't just stand there like that!" Someone angrily yelled, his voice hoarse, thick with pain. "The shelter has collapsed. People are dying right in front of you. Oh, God!"

"Oh, my God! I think it's the public shelter. There are so many people in there!" the woman blurted out.

"I'll have to go give them a hand. You go home first. I'll follow!" I said.

I released her hand and ran hastily after the crowd. As I ran, I turned back, motioned with my hand and shouted:

"Go home! Wait there for me!" Near the site of the explosion, before I was to plow into the smoking remnants of the freshly destroyed houses, I turned back one more time. After a hellish night, it was the last glimpse I had of my beloved and illusory figure.

But it shouldn't have been the last time. I should have been able to return to that same house, to the same room where I was the previous night, to see this woman again. It was morning, a long time after the all-clear signals. I followed the trolley tracks, retracing my path from the night before, to go back to her house.

I thought nothing at first when I had to step aside to dodge a trolley. It was cold and the street was empty. The old, rusty trolley lunged forward; the bell silent; its steel wheels shrieking, throwing off sparks; the engine making an ear-shattering racket. But as it passed me, I gave a little start, as if my heart had just been whipped.

The street was straight, endless, without intersections. On each side of the street, the same houses crowded into each other, all identical, monotonous: a gloomy, grouchy façade shaded by a rusty tin roof; three steps leading to a single door. In front of every house was a cement hole. Since the trolley, my only clue, was gone, all I knew for sure was which side of the street the house was on. Everything looked the same, the same uneven, broken sidewalk, with puddles of stagnant water; the same walls and leaky roofs; the same arjun trees and light poles.

Although I had no time to spare, I stalked back and forth on that street, brooding over my failure. I stared into the houses and at the faces of people coming out. By the time another trolley came clanking by, I had to give up. With a face still covered in soot and ash, limbs all scratched, and wearing tatters stained with blotches of blood from the night's victims, I trudged dejectedly along the trolley tracks toward my destination on the outskirts of the city.

After the war, on my rare visits to Hanoi, I would always return to that same street. I would simply walk down it, not to find anything or go anywhere. The last time I got off at Hang Co train station, I could no longer recognize my old street. Hanoi had abolished the trolleys. The streets were glamorous; the houses beautiful; life happy . . .

There may come a day when people will have a hard time imagining a period when this city went through what I saw twenty years ago, when I was a very young man.

Translated by Linh Dinh

REFLECTIONS OF SPRING

Duong Thu Huong

*I*t's not because of that evening. But since then, thoughts of her hadn't left his mind. They would linger for a while, then rush at him like a gust of wind, throwing his thoughts into chaos and disrupting his equanimity, leaving behind vague and anguished longings. That evening, he was returning to Hanoi from a midland province. An economic planner, he was used to these long, tedious trips. Dozing in his seat on the bus, he was awoken by loud clanking sounds coming from the engine. The driver lifted the hood and moaned:

"Can't make it to Hanoi this evening. The radiator is broken . . ."

The passengers got off the bus to walk around and to breathe in the pleasant air of the midland area. Yellow fields ran to the horizon. In the distance, one could see the uneven peaks of dark green hills, like a clique of moss-covered snails resting on a carpet of rice paddies. The yellow of ripe rice was pale in the fading sun, but it flared up in spots, as if still soaked in light. At the edge of the road, the harvested field had a soft pink glow, as gentle as adolescent love. The autumn breeze made him feel light-headed: He was free from projects, reports, criticisms, approvals—all hindrances and distractions. It was an unusual feeling, this clarity. He walked briskly along.

By the side of the road was a row of houses. Their uneven roofs and white walls gave a strong warmth to the landscape. Butted up against each other, the houses were fronted by a mishmash of verandas in different styles. In the small yards were tree stumps and piles of bricks. Nearby, pigeon coops perched on tree branches. At the base of a mound of shiny yellow straw, smelling of harvest, an old hen led her chicks, cluck-clucking, searching for food. A crude red and green sign announced a bicycle repair shop. In front, a dangling flat tire wobbled with each gust of wind. Bunches of bananas, suspended from hooks, hovered over the heads of diners in the cheap restaurants.

The serenity and melancholic air of the small town enchanted him. He didn't know what he was thinking, but he walked up and down the streets admiring the familiar views, especially the shrubs and poinciana plants behind the houses. The yellow flowers bloomed in the quiet evening.

"Uncle, come in for a drink. We have country rice pies and sticky-rice cakes."

An old woman behind a small glass display case leaned forward to greet her customer. He was a little surprised; it had been a long time since he heard such a natural, friendly greeting from a shopkeeper. He walked in and sat down on a long bench. He didn't know why he had walked in; he wasn't hungry, thirsty, or in need of a smoke from the water pipe. But he had a strong intuition he was waiting for something. It was vague yet urgent. His heart beat anxiously. The shopkeeper leisurely poured out a bowl of green tea for her customer. Then she sat back, chewed her betel nut, and said nothing. He raised the bowl of tea, took a sip and looked around. A gust of wind whirled some yellow leaves. From a distance, they looked like tiny gold grains that nature had generously scattered.

He had known all of this at one time. They were images

from his past, although he wasn't aware of it. He felt increasingly uneasy.

"Grandma, should I make more rice wafers?"

A girl's voice echoed from inside the house. The sound of her voice startled him. He almost got up to rudely peer into the other room. But he restrained himself. The shop owner's granddaughter came out from the back:

"I baked ten more rice wafers, Grandma. There's none left in the basket!"

Seeing him, the girl stepped back cautiously. The old woman opened the bag and took out a bunch of small rice wafers. "Bake twenty small ones for Grandma. They're easier to sell." The girl answered "yes" in a low voice and leaned over the earthenware basin to blow into the fire. The white ashes flew up, danced in the air and gently landed on her shiny black hair. Her teenage face was smooth and ruddy as a ripe fruit. Her nose was straight and graceful. She had a simple haircut, parted down the middle. He couldn't take his eyes off her; his heart beat excitedly.

"This is it!"

This unspoken sentiment had echoed within him as the girl came out . . . Twenty-three years ago, when he was in the tenth grade and a boarder in a small town, there was a similarly pretty and well-behaved girl. The same earthenware basin with red coals throwing off cinders, the same ruddy cheeks and round wrists . . . but the girl from his memory had a long hollow trace on her forehead. There were the same poinciana flowers and tiny yellow leaves, scattered by gusts of wind, dotting the ground in autumn, when sounds from the radio mixed with rustling from the unharvested rice paddies and the incessant noises of insects—the lazy, forlorn music of a small town.

It was odd how deeply buried these memories were. He was very poor then. Each month, his mother would send him only three *dong* for pocket money and 10 kilograms of rice. But he studied harder than all the other boys in his class, who called him a bookworm. The pretty girl lived next door to the house where he rented his room. She used to lean her arms against the fence and listen to him memorize poems out loud. Her mother was a food vendor; she would squat in front of the earthenware basin to bake rice wafers for her mother. At night, when he studied, she also lit an oil lamp and sat under the carambola tree to do her homework. At 10 o'clock, as his face was still buried in a book, she would hoist a carrying pole onto her shoulder to go get water for her family. She was a good student and never needed his help. Still, she would look at him admiringly as he diagrammed a geometric problem, or as he closed his eyes and recited, smooth as soup, a long poem. By the time she came back with the water, he would be ready for bed. He was so hungry he had to literally tighten his belt. It was then she would bring him a piping hot rice wafer. The two of them didn't say much. Usually, he just smiled:

"What luck, my stomach was growling."

He never bothered to thank her. But they both felt that they needed to see each other, look at each other's faces and talk about nothing. Neither of them dared to ask too deeply about the other. Truth is, there was nothing more to ask . . . Her piping hot wafers; the hollow trace on her forehead; the bright face; the understanding looks when he was homesick, sitting all bunched up during cold, rainy evenings.

He suddenly remembered all these things. All of them. He now understood what he had been waiting for that evening. It had arrived. That beautiful, sweet, distant memory. A memory, buried for more than twenty years, awakened suddenly by a gust of wind.

The young girl, who was fanning the fire, looked up: "Grandma, I've finished ten . . . Give me a hand . . ."

She gave the stack of yellow wafers to the old woman and glanced curiously at the strange customer. He rotated the tea bowl in his hands while staring at her. She became flustered and clumsily swatted a lump of coal to the ground with her fan. She picked it up immediately, threw it back into the basin, then blew on her two fingers to cool them off, her brows knit in a frown.

"Now she looks like a twelve-year-old. The other girl was older, and more pretty," he thought.

Once, he didn't have enough money to buy textbooks. It wasn't clear how she found out. That night, along with the wafers, she also gave him a small envelope. He opened it: inside was a small stack of bills. The notes were so new you could smell the aroma of paper and ink. It was her New Year's money. He sat motionless. It looked like she had been hoarding it for ten months and hadn't touched it. "But what did I do that day?" After graduating, he was preoccupied with taking the university admissions exam. After his acceptance, knowing he was going away, he excitedly took care of the paperwork, merrily said goodbye to everyone, then took a train straight for Hanoi.

"Why didn't I say goodbye to the girl? No, I was about to, but it was getting too close to my departure date. I was rushed by my relatives. And intimidated by such an opportunity . . ."

And after that? A fresh environment; a strange city; life's frantic rhythm made him dizzy; bright lights; streetcars; the first parties where he felt awkward, provincial, out of place; teahouses; the blackboard in the classroom; new girlfriends . . .

"Eat the hot rice wafers, Uncle. It's aromatic in your mouth. In Hanoi, you don't get country treats like this." The old shopkeeper gave him a small rice wafer. Its fluffy surface was speckled with golden sesame seeds—very appetizing. He broke off a small piece and put it in his mouth. It was a taste he had long forgotten about.

"I used to think rice wafers were the most delicious food on earth," he thought. He remembered studying at night, particularly nights when he had to memorize history and biology lessons—two damnable subjects, when he was so hungry waiting for her footsteps near the fence that his mouth could taste the deliciously baked rice flour and the fatty sesame seeds . . . that taste and smell . . . and her wet eyes looking at him, as she rested her arms on the windowsill and smiled:

"I knew you were hungry, Brother. I get pretty hungry at night also. Mother told me to go into town tomorrow to buy cassava so we can have something extra to eat at night." The next day she brought him pieces of boiled cassava. At eighteen, eating them, he also thought her boiled cassava was the most delicious food on earth. Once, she gave him cassava wrapped in banana leaves. It was steaming hot. As he yanked his arms back, she grabbed both his hands and the hot cassava. She let go immediately, her eyes wide in astonishment. As for him, he was as dizzy as he had been that one holiday morning, when he had drunk too much sweet wine . . .

"I really did love her back then . . . I really did love . . ." Then why hadn't he gone back to that town to find her? Finished with his studies, he was assigned a job by the government. Then he had to apply for housing. Then he was involved with a female colleague. Life worries. There was a secret agreement, then the marriage license. That was his wife, unattractive yet dogged in her pursuit of his love, who used every trick imaginable to make him yield to the harsh demands of necessity . . . And then what? Children. Problems at work. A promotion. Steps forward and backward. Years spent overseas to get a doctorate degree . . . Everything has to be tabulated.

"Is the wafer good, Uncle?" the old woman asked.

"Very good, Grandmother," he answered. Crumbs fell onto his knees and he brushed them off. The old hen came over, cluck clucking for her chicks to come pick the crumbs.

"Why didn't I look for her? Why did I . . . Well, I had to achieve, at all costs, the planning targets for operative 038 . . . And, to raise my kids, I had to teach to supplement my income. My daughters don't resemble me; they are like their mother, ugly, stuck-up . . . But do I love my wife? Probably not . . . Most likely not. I've never tingled because of that woman like I did years ago waiting for the sounds of the little girl's footsteps. Especially in the afternoon, with everyone gone, when she washed her hair—with her cheeks dripping wet and strands of hair nappy on her temples. As she dried her hair, one hand on the fence, she would smile because she knew I was secretly admiring her . . . As for my wife, there's never any suspense; I never look forward to seeing her, nor feel empty when we're apart. Back then, going home to get rice, how I anticipated seeing the little girl again, even after only a day . . . My wife needed a husband and she found me. As for me . . ."

This thought nearly drove him mad. He stood up abruptly. The girl fanning the fire stared at him, her eyes black as coal, a deep dimple on one cheek.

He paid the old woman and started walking toward the bus. He wanted to return to Hanoi immediately. He wanted to forget these thoughts . . .

But the bus wasn't fixed until 2 in the morning. They returned to Hanoi by dawn. He returned to his daily life, to his daily business and worries . . . The thoughts of the little girl never left him. They would circle back like the hands on a watch.

"Why didn't I go find her back then? I surely would have had a different wife. And who knows . . ." The little girl is thirty-eight now, but to him she's still fifteen. She is his true love, but why do people only find out these things twenty years later? He flicked the cigarette ashes into the fancy pink ashtray and watched the tiny embers slowly die. On the bed, his wife sleepily raised her head:

"Why are you up so late, dear? Are you admiring me?"

"Yes, yes, I'm admiring you," he answered, squashing the cigarette butt in the ashtray. His wife had just bought an embroidered dress from Thailand and had asked what he thought of it three times already.

"Go to bed, dear."

"I still have work to do."

"I wonder where the little girl is living now? What is she doing? Maybe I can take a bus there tomorrow. No, no, that's not possible." He saw clearly that to walk away silently twenty-three years ago was wrong. How could he possibly go back, when he had dismissed love so easily?

He retrieved the cigarette butt and lit it again. The ember returned to his lips.

A garden full of shades. Carambolas on the ground like fallen stars. And the smell of ripe carambolas. And her wet eyes. Her head tilted as she stood near the fence . . .

"But I was very shy then. I didn't dare to make any vow . . . Stop denying it—it is useless when it comes to love." He knew he had loved her and she had loved him, but he was impatient to get out of there because he was dazzled by his own prospects. During the last hectic days, he did brood over a petty calculation. He did plan to . . . but never realized it.

"It wasn't like that, because . . .

"Sure it was.

"It wasn't like that . . .

"Yes, and you can't be forgiven . . ."

He threw the cigarette butt into the ashtray and flopped into an armchair. The polyester-covered cushions weren't as comfortable as usual. He stood up again, went to the window and pushed the glass panes open.

"It's cold, honey," his wife shrieked.

He didn't turn around, but answered gruffly:

"Then use the blanket."

Many stars lit up the night sky. He suddenly smelled the scent of fresh straw, of harvest. This familiar smell shrouded the neighborhood, a fragrance to stir one's soul. The poinciana flowers bloomed in the evening . . . Everything revived— vague, spurious, yet stark enough to make him bitter. His head was spinning.

He lit a second cigarette and slapped himself on the forehead.

"What is going on?"

There was no answer. Only a rising tremolo of rice stalks and leaves rustling. Again, the swirling sky over the crown of the carambola tree; her smooth, firm arms on the windowsill as she smiled at him. White teeth like two rows of corn. His love had returned, right now, within him. He walked uncon- sciously to the mirror. His hair had begun to gray. Lines were etched all over his cheeks. Behind the glasses, his eyes had started to become lifeless. He drew deeply on the cigarette then exhaled. The pale blue smoke billowed shapelessly, like the confusions in his life.

His report contained many interesting proposals and was very well received, a complete success. Both his bosses and rivals were equally impressed. He himself didn't know how he had managed to do it. All the endless nights, walking back and forth, watching smoke rise then evaporate, when he had thought of her. She, the object of his true love—a love not shared, not articulated, what does it all add up to? But these soothing, melancholic memories had kept him awake at night, and he had written his report during these late hours, as he tried to recover what had disappeared from his life.

At the conference, people were admiring the exhibits illustrating his proposals. He had succeeded almost completely. Even his enemies were congratulating him. He smiled, shook hands and thanked everybody before slipping out into the hallway. Alone.

His closest colleague ran out to find him. The man looked him in the eye and said:

"The newspaper photographers are waiting for you. What's wrong, Brother? Are you in love?"

"Me, in love?" he chuckled, then snapped, "Me, love?! Are you mad? Me still in love . . . a steel-and-cement man, a . . . and with my hair turning . . ."

He didn't finish his sentence, but rushed out the gate. He walked down a little lane. For some reason, his eyes were stinging, as if smoke had blown into them. Where's that hamlet, that town? With pigeon coops and piles of straw in the yards. And poinciana flowers blooming in the evening sun. And the windswept rice paddies, with their ripe stalks rustling. And the harvested fields glowing, a soft pink, distant . . .

Translated by Nguyen Nguyet Cam and Linh Dinh

WITHOUT A KING

Nguyen Huy Thiep

1. The Household

*S*inh had been a daughter-in-law in Old Kien's household for several years now. When she came, she brought with her four sets of summer clothes, a winter shirt, two sweaters, a flower-patterned blanket, a copper skillet, a flour tub, a two-liter hotwater bottle, a basin for bathing, a dozen towels—in short, a sum of money, since her parents were rice-dealers in the Xanh market.

Sinh's husband, Can, was a disabled vet. They met by accident. Both were hiding under the same eaves during a rainstorm. This story has already been recorded. (Just goes to show how inquisitive our writers are!) As told, it was a simple love scene, pure, without an ulterior motive. Life is a tangible object, tranquil, attractive, deserving of passion, etc.

Can was the eldest son. Then came his four younger brothers, who were born one or two years apart. Doai worked for the Education Department; Khiem was a butcher for a food supplier; Kham was a student at the university. Ton, the youngest one, was mentally ill, his body puny, weird-looking.

There were six people in Old Kien's family. All men. Mrs. Nhon, Old Kien's wife, had died eleven years earlier, when Old Kien was fifty-three, an awkward age to marry again or to not marry again. Old Kien chose the lesser inconvenience and did nothing . . .

Old Kien's house looked into the street. He fixed bicycles for a living. Can cut hair (when he first met Sinh, he told her he "handled accounts"). Having received a modest education (her father taught school, her mother sold rice), Sinh was not one to be narrow-minded. Moreover, she could be quite liberal in her manners. Her limited education (Sinh only had a general degree) did not get in her way. With women, learning contributes little to their supernatural strength, a fact that does not need to be proven.

As a new bride, in the beginning, Sinh was a little startled by the house's liberal climate. There was absolutely no decorum at the dinner table: six men, all bare-chested and in shorts, chattering away, gulping and slurping like dragons. Sinh took care of the three daily meals. The heavy jobs she did not have to do. There was Ton to help out. All day long, Ton did the laundry and washed the floor. He couldn't do much else. Always with a plastic bucket and a rag, he'd wash the floor every few hours. He hated dirt. Whenever anyone changed clothes he did the laundry, and did it extremely well, including the drying. He spoke little and only giggled when addressed, with clunky, terse answers. Often, he'd sing as he worked, a song he learned, God knows when, from the drinking crowd:

Aha . . . Without a king
Drunk from morning till evening
The days and months are nothing
Me and myself together
Drunk from evening till morn . . .

With absolute devotion, Ton always tried to help Sinh out. All her little needs he'd try to fulfill. In the middle of the night, if Sinh said, "Some prunes would be good," there would be prunes immediately. Where he got the money, or when he bought them, no one knew.

In the house, Sinh dreaded Old Kien the most, then Khiem. Old Kien was cantankerous all day long. No one liked him. He made money. He argued with everyone out of habit, in the meanest language. With Doai, for example, he'd say: "Is that you? The civil servant? More useless than a leper, and illiterate, good only at taking bribes!" Or Kham, who was in his second year at the university: "Parasites! What learning? A waste of good rice!" With Can, he was not so belligerent, occasionally even giving him a compliment, although the old man's compliments were more like insults: "Amazing, this job of shaving whiskers and cleaning out ear wax, humiliating to be sure but still a good source of money!" Khiem was the only one he left alone.

Khiem was a big guy, aloof, with a short temper. Each night, as he came home (he worked the night shift), he'd bring either meat or intestines. Rarely did he come home empty-handed. Doai often said (behind Khiem's back, of course): "That guy will end up in jail sooner or later. I can see it. No less than six years. Weird how they've left him alone so far, stealing half a ton of meat annually!"

It appeared that Khiem did not think much of his two older brothers. With Can, he'd always pay for his haircuts. Khiem said: "Don't treat me differently, Brother. If I make you work, I have the right to pay." Can cringed: "You act like we're not family." Khiem said: "Family nothing. If you don't want my money, I'll go somewhere else, make some other guy clean out my ear wax . . . Yo, careful with that knife. Don't shave off my mustache." Can didn't know what to say, and had to accept Khiem's money. Sinh told her husband: "You take his money, he'll look down on you." Can replied: "I'm still the oldest. He can't look down on me."

Doai, Khiem considered an enemy. But Doai was too smooth, and Khiem couldn't pick fights with him. Before work, Doai always put some rice into his bag, and a few pieces of meat. Doai said: "This little bit of protein means 2,000 calories, enough to last me all day. Thanks to Khiem, we're all quick and clever in this household." Khiem asked: "Quick and clever how?" Doai said: "Like you, for instance. You're clever with people and quick with meat." Khiem, all pissed off, foamed at the mouth.

Sinh's appearance in this household was like rain falling on parched earth. During the first few months, Old Kien stopped arguing with his children. Can was the happiest. He was fast with the scissors and always very cordial toward the customers. He decided to increase the fees for a haircut from 30 to 50, an ear job from 10 to 20, a shampoo from 20 to 30, a shave from 10 to 20. Profit increased. The family budget, which Can controlled, became more relaxed. Doai, noticing the jump in daily expenditures, was alarmed at first, but calmed down when no one said anything about his own contribution. As for Khiem, it remained as before, never a dime, only intestines or two kilograms of meat daily. After ten days of intestines, Sinh freaked out and said to her husband: "If Khiem brings back more intestines tomorrow, I'll take it to the market and exchange them for something else." Can smiled, stroked his wife's soft body and said: "Whatever you wish, Madam."

2. In the Morning

Normally, Khiem was the first to get up in the morning. He set the alarm clock for 1. When it went off, he would get up immediately, brush his teeth, then leave on his bicycle. Ton locked the door behind him. Doai, disrupted from sleep, bitched: "Truly the working hours of a criminal." At 3 o'clock, Old Kien got up, plugged in the electric stove to boil water for tea. The outlet was faulty and had been fixed several times, but every few days someone still got a good jolt. When Old Kien got a good jolt, he blurted: "Your ancestors! You guys want to get rid of me, but there's a God above, with eyes, and I'll be around for a long time!" From his bed, Doai yelped: "I don't know about elsewhere, but in this household, the green leaves fall down before the yellow ones." Old Kien countered: "Your mother! What a way to talk to your father! Who hired you to work for the Education Department?" Doai laughed: "They checked my family history. Three spotless generations, as clear as a mirror." Old Kien mumbled: "Absolutely. I don't know about you guys, but starting with me and going backward, no one has ever done anything disgraceful in this household." Doai said: "Sure. To jack up the price of patching a tire from 10 to 30 is really charitable." Old Kien said: "Your mother! What thoughts go through your mind when you lift that bowl of rice to your lips every day?" Kham moaned: "Spare me, Brother Doai, have a little pity, I've got a big test in philosophy today." Doai said: "Philosophy is a luxury for bookworms. See the plastic rosary on Sinh's neck. That's philosophy." Kham did not answer. The house quieted down for about a hour before becoming noisy again. It was 4 in the morning, the hour when Sinh got up to cook.

Sinh measured six and a half cans of rice. Can stooped to clean the vegetables. Kham said: "A beautiful pair. Anything I can do?" Sinh said: "The pork fat from yesterday is covered with ants, see if you can get rid of those ants." Kham said: "In our country, we must be the leading family as far as the amount of pig intestines consumed per head. I've done a rough estimate. In a single year, Khiem has brought back 260 sets of intestines." Doai said: "Little brother, that guy is a godsend for our family. Correct me if I'm wrong, but that butcher job is worth ten of our college degrees."

Old Kien opened shop. A woman carrying a pot of sticky rice stuck her head in: "Breakfast for you, sir?" Old Kien rubbed his hands together: "My God, this is a business. With a broad like you first thing in the morning to bring me bad luck, how can I make any money?" The woman selling sticky rice said: "I've never sold a dime's worth of sticky rice to this old guy." Can stroked his blade against the calfskin, mumbling: "It would be good if I could cut ten heads today."

The food was brought out, Sinh and Kham sat near the rice

pot. Kham stirred the rice. Sinh said: "It's still too hot, no one will be able to eat it." Kham said: "Don't worry, Sister. The Si's all have mouths of steel." Sinh said: "After you, Father. And after you, Can, and all my brothers." Doai said: "Customs vary according to the household, and in this one, there's no need for ceremony. Stir me a bowl, Kham." Kham said: "What speed. I've just gotten through two scoops."

Doai said: "I've been eating group meals since I was fourteen, I'm used to eating fast. When in college, there was a guy who could eat six bowls in a minute and a half. Scary, huh?" Old Kien said: "Intellectuals these days talk about nothing." Kham smiled: "Isn't there an old saying, 'food before virtue'?" Old Kien asked: "What virtues have you guys attained?" Doai finished eating, stood up, arched his back: "This is a topic for a debate. I suspect whoever made up that saying in the old days didn't know shit about virtues. The guy should have said, 'food before compassion.' As in human compassion, my fellow countrymen." Can chuckled: "You've got a lot of compassion, my brother." Doai stared at his sister-in-law's cleavage, where there was a button open on her shirt, and pondered: "Compassion, compassion, revealed compassion is making me dreamy." Sinh turned red and discreetly buttoned herself a moment later.

Sinh cleaned up. Old Kien sat and drank tea. Kham put on a pair of jeans and a T-shirt, with the inscription "Walt Disney Productions" on it. Kham said: "Brother Can, give me a 50." Can said: "I have no money." Kham said: "Father, give me a 50." Old Kien said: "You sit down and patch that tire over there, then I'll give you some money." Kham cringed: "But I'll be late for class." Without answering, Old Kien opened his toolbox and started busying himself. Kham walked his bicycle to the door, paused to think for a moment, then walked back into the house. He went into the back room, looked around to make sure no one was looking, then shoveled a can and a half of uncooked rice into his bag before sneaking out again.

Sinh put the pots away in the kitchen. Doai followed

behind her, to pack a lunch for work. His hand touched Sinh's back. Doai said: "My sister's body, as soft as a noodle." Sinh backed up, startled: "Hell, Doai, what was that?" Doai said: "Boy, a little joke and what a reaction." He left the kitchen.

Ton lugged the water bucket, assiduously washing the floor, singing: "Aha . . . Without a king . . ."

A man walked in for a haircut. Can asked: "What style, Uncle?" The customer said: "Cut it close. But be careful, I've got a lump near the top of my head."

Doai finished dressing and walked his bicycle out. At the door, he turned to address Can: "The day after tomorrow is Mother's death anniversary, tell Khiem to get a good cut of meat. I already gave Sinh a hundred." Can said: "I know already."

3. The Death Anniversary

For his wife's death anniversary, Old Kien had five trays of food prepared. From her family, there was Mr. Vy who came from Phuc Yen to attend. Mr. Vy was a retired civil servant whose retirement checks were equal to a government employee's of the third rank. Mr. Vy had many children, was poor, and came with only ten calabashes and a bottle of white wine as presents. From the city came Old Kien's sister's family. She sold dry goods, and her husband, Mr. Hien, was a tinsmith. The Hiens had five children, boys and girls. Other guests included Mr. Minh, a manager in Doai's office. Kham brought home three classmates—a girl named My Lan, a girl named My Trinh, and a boy called Viet Hung, who wore silver glasses and had lips as red as a woman's.

All the guests had arrived by about 10. Can brought a tray of food to the altar, lit three incense sticks, turned around and said: "You pray, Father." Old Kien, wearing a pair of colonial work pants and a white short-sleeved shirt with three pockets, his hair slick from sprayed water, walked in front of the altar and muttered: "The Socialist People's Republic of

Vietnam, in the year . . . To God, to Buddha, to my ancestors, to the angels, to my wife, whose name is Ngo Thi Nhon. I invite you all to share this modest meal with me. I, Nguyen Si Kien, sixty-four years old, a resident of 29, district . . . My sons are Can, Doai, Khiem, Kham, Ton. My daughter-in-law is Sinh. We all beg you to protect us, to give us health and to assist us in our business endeavors." After saying his prayer, Old Kien turned to Mr. Vy: "You go and bow once to your sister." Mr. Vy wore a political cadre suit in the Ton Trung Son style, buttoned right to the neck and very dignified. Mr. Vy said: "We Party members have no gods. After forty years of following the Revolution, there's not an altar in my house, and I don't even know how to say a prayer anymore." Old Kien was silent, his eyes red. Mr. Vy walked to the altar, stood still, and bowed his head. Old Kien wiped his eyes and said: "Now one after another, whoever wants to bow can go ahead and bow." Mrs. Hien, after arranging on the altar some hell notes, fake gold, a paper suit, kneeled and prostrated herself three times, with her forehead touching the floor. Can also bowed three times. Can said: "You do it, Doai." Doai was chopping chicken, his hands all greasy. He left them like that and ran to the altar, where he bowed furiously: "Dearest Mother, help me to go study abroad, get a Cub motorcycle." Mr. Vy smiled: "Which country are you going to, my nephew?" Doai said: "That will depend on the mustachioed guy in the plaid shirt over there." Mr. Minh heard this and said: "How am I responsible for you going somewhere?" Doai said: "That's how it is, you're my boss. If you turn your back, I'm dead." Mr. Minh said: "Keep up the good work. I'll take care of you." Doai said: "How can you tell what's good or bad when you're working for the government? Just remember that Doai here has always been good to you."

Sinh was busy in the kitchen. In her room, Kham was showing his three friends a photo album, with pictures of himself in it, including his baby pictures. My Lan said: "You were a cute baby, Kham." Kham said: "My kid will be just as

cute, maybe even cuter, with a birthmark right on the chin."
My Lan turned red, rubbed the birthmark on her chin and
rained punches down Kham's back. Viet Hung said: "This pic-
ture was taken when you went for training, right?" Kham
said: "Yeah." Viet Hung complimented: "Real sharp." My Lan
asked: "That's the time you stole cassavas and were caught
by the self-defense force, right?" Kham turned red. He said:
"Talking trash. You're guilty of slandering a comrade. I'll
make sure you pay a penalty." My Lan asked: "What penalty?"
Kham said: "You'll know later on tonight." Everyone
laughed.

Doai looked in, gestured toward Kham. Doai said: "Set the
table." Kham asked: "Eat already?" Doai didn't answer. Kham
followed Doai into the kitchen. Doai asked: "The one with the
birthmark is your girlfriend?" Kham said: "Yes." Doai asked:
"And who's that sweet-smelling heroine?" Kham laughed:
"That's My Trinh, her father is Mr. Daylight, the owner of the
electric store." Doai asked: "How's that guy with her?" Kham
said: "Nothing yet." Doai said: "I'll prick her."

Kham carried the tray. Sinh said: "Yell if something's
missing." After Kham left, Doai said: "A little love's missing.
Please give me a little love, Sinh." Sinh said: "Freak. Go into
the house and ask Kham's two girlfriends." Doai said: "How
can those two sluts equal you?" Sinh said: "Get out." Doai
said: "Your old man, Can, may look like a field crab but he
does have an attitude." Sinh said: "I'll tell Can about you."
Doai said: "I'm not afraid." After saying that, he nudged close
and kissed Sinh slightly on the cheek. Sinh pushed him off.
Doai gasped: "I'll say it ahead of time. Sooner or later, I'll
sleep with you at least once." After saying that, he left. Sinh
burst into sobs.

Can came in, saw his wife's eyes all red, asked: "What's
wrong?" Sinh said: "It's because of this lousy kitchen." Can
said: "Bring some hot water into the house. There's none left."
Sinh said: "Do I have six hands and three heads?" Can stared:
"Is that a way to talk? This house is not like that! And how

come these dishes are not washed?" After saying that, he knocked over the stack of bowls and walked out. The bowls crashed. Sinh burst out crying.

There were three trays served during the first sitting. After eating, some guests went home. Then there were two more trays served for the second sitting. By then it was 2 in the afternoon. In the middle of eating, Khiem came in, very sullen, and greeted no one. Kham said: "Sit down with us and enjoy yourself, Brother Khiem." The two girls, My Lan and My Trinh, chirped their invitations. Everyone held their chopsticks.

Old Kien, drunk, nodded off in bed and slavered onto the rattan mat. Doai excused himself to take Mr. Vy to the bus station for the Phu Yen evening departure.

Khiem asked: "Where's Ton?" Kham said: "He's around somewhere. Come and eat, Brother, we're waiting." Khiem said: "You guys go ahead." Kham said: "We'll eat all right. That guy has a fuckin' attitude." My Trinh said: "He looks like Tarzan."

Khiem went into the kitchen to ask Sinh: "Where's Ton?" Sinh said: "I've been busy since early this morning and have totally forgotten about him. I don't know where he is." Khiem dumped a heavy sack onto the counter. Sinh asked: "More intestines?" Khiem didn't answer, walked into the house, peered into Sinh's room to see Can snoring. Khiem shoved the door open, asked Can: "Where's Ton?" Can sat up: "What time is it?" Khiem asked: "Where's Ton?" Can said: "We had guests. Not a good idea to have him running around. I locked him up in the shed next to the toilet!" Khiem picked up the ashtray on the table and threw it at Can's face. Can went "Oi" once and keeled over. Khiem lunged forward and kicked Can repeatedly. Kham ran in, pushed Khiem away. Sinh ran in, panic-stricken, and said: "What was that?" Khiem brushed her aside.

The shed next to the toilet, once a pigsty, was now used to store firewood. There was a wooden door. Someone had put a lock on it that wasn't there yesterday. Khiem yanked on the lock, no good. Khiem used a crowbar to break the lock. The door opened. Ton, with a black face, black arms, and black legs, bared his teeth in a smile. Khiem yelled: "Get out."

Ton dragged his lame legs into the house. Seeing the dirty floor, he immediately fetched the water bucket and the rag.

Kham's friends tittered their goodbyes then left. Kham walked his bicycle out after them. Before he left, he grabbed a few cigarettes from the table and put them in his shirt pocket.

Old Kien sobered up, noticed the empty house, asked: "Where's everybody?" Sinh brought some bean threads for Ton to eat. Ton was hungry, ate three or four bowls in a row, spilling bean threads onto the floor. Khiem walked his bicycle out, he ate nothing. Can clutched his own chest, coughed furiously, and spat out a broken tooth, a corner of his mouth smeared with blood. Can waved a fist in front of his father's face: "You better throw that guy out of the house before I kill him!" Old Kien said: "You guys go ahead and kill each other. It will only make me happy." After saying that, he held the broken lock in his hands, mumbling: "All morning it took to put this lock on. A waste of 100 *dong*."

4. Evening

By the time Sinh finished the dishes, it was 3 o' clock. Sinh went into her room for a change of clothes to take a shower. Suddenly, she panicked and called for Can. Can asked: "What?" Sinh said: "I left a ring in the needle box this morning, have you taken it?" Can said: "No." Sinh asked: "Anyone come into this room?" Can said: "No."

Doai walked his bicycle in, noticed stuff everywhere, asked: "What's up?" Can grimaced: "Did you come into this room?" Doai said: "No." Can said: "Sinh's missing a ring." Doai said: "Ask Father." Old Kien cursed: "Your mother! You think I stole the ring?" Doai was silent, thought for a moment, then said: "This morning Kham and his three friends sat in this room. I suspect the guy with the glasses and the lipsticked lips. His eyes were extremely cunning."

Luckily, Kham came in at that moment. Can said: "Your friend stole Sinh's ring." Kham turned ashen: "Who said?" Can said: "I saw him do it." Kham said: "Why didn't you catch him in the act? When we were out just now, he insisted on going home. Now we have to go to his house to get it back. If he doesn't want to return it, we'll beat the shit out of him." Can said: "I'll go with you." The two of them walked their bicycles out. Old Kien said: "Take the hammer with you! But don't hit him in the head. If the guy dies, you'll go to jail for life."

Doai climbed into bed to read the paper. Sinh cleaned up a little and then got ready for her shower. She carried two buckets of water into the shower stall, closed the door.

Old Kien was fidgeting around in the kitchen, heard water splashing inside the shower, sighed, and walked toward the house. After a few steps, Old Kien turned around, reentered the kitchen, grabbed a chair, stepped on top of it, held his breath, and peered into the shower. Inside the shower stall, Sinh stood naked.

Doai, drifting into sleep, noticed Ton tugging on his shirt, sat up, and said: "What?" Ton rubbed his hands together, took Doai into the kitchen, pointed to Old Kien standing on tiptoes on the chair. Doai grimaced and gave Ton a hard slap on the face. Ton fell, face first, onto the water bucket with a rag. Old Kien hopped quickly from his chair and hid near the door. A moment later he said: "Why hit him?" Doai said: "I hit him because he has no manners." Old Kien raised his voice: "Then I suppose you have manners?" Doai gritted his teeth and whispered: "I have no manners either, but I don't peek at naked women." Old Kien stayed silent.

Doai went into the house, poured a cup of wine. Old Kien helped Ton get up. Ton fetched the water bucket and squatted down to wash the floor. Old Kien went into the house and said to Doai: "Pour me a cup." After emptying his cup, Old Kien said: "You're educated but still stupid. Now I'll talk to you man-to-man." Doai said: "I won't forgive." Old Kien said: "I don't need it. A man needn't be ashamed for having a prick . . ." Doai sat in silence, drank another cup then sighed: "True enough." Old Kien said: "It's humiliating to be human." Doai asked: "Then why didn't you remarry?" Old Kien cursed: "Your mother! If I'd only thought about myself, would you guys have all this?" Doai poured another cup, asked: "More wine, Father?" Old Kien turned his face into the shadow, shook his head. Doai said: "I'm sorry, Father." Old Kien said: "Now you're behaving like an actor on TV."

Ton washed the floor, noticed the ring beneath the cabinet and gave it to Sinh. Sinh was elated. Doai held the ring up to the light, said: "Half a karat, maximum." Sinh said: "It's an heirloom from my mother, her entire life's savings." Old Kien said: "Shit, with Can picking a fight at that guy's house, we will all look ridiculous."

Can and Kham came back just before dark. Both looked as if they had just crawled out of the gutter, all slimy, pathetic. Doai laughed: "Got a good beating?" Can did not answer. Kham said: "They keep two German shepherds in that house, no way to get in." Doai said: "That'll teach you to act tough before you know what's happening."

Old Kien said: "We found the ring." Can asked: "Where?" Old Kien said: "Your wife kept it inside the hem of her pants, that's where." Can said: "You bitch!" After saying that, he gave Sinh a hard slap on the face that made her see stars. Can was about to hit her again when Doai shoved him out of the way. Doai stood in front of Sinh, shielding her, with his hand poised on a knife, and hissed: "Go away! If you touch her again, I'll stab you immediately."

Sinh leaned her face against the bedpost and cried out: "Oh God . . . Why am I humiliated like this?"

Old Kien asked Kham: "Did you bring the hammer back?" Kham got testy: "I almost lost my life to two German shepherds, who cares about hammers and pliers?" Old Kien said: "There goes another hundred."

5. New Year's Day

Soon it was New Year's Day. On December 15, Old Kien went to the bank to withdraw the interest from his savings. Old Kien bought a shirt for Ton and a pair of socks for Sinh. What was left of the money he gave to Can. Kham said: "Father dotes only on his daughter-in-law and his youngest son."

Khiem had to travel to different towns to buy pigs and would be gone for days on end. It must have been hard work, he would leave at 11 every night and not return until the next afternoon, his entire body reeking of pig manure. Although he'd fall asleep as soon as he got home, his eyes were still bloodshot and sunken.

Can also had many customers. From 6 in the morning until 10 at night, there would always be someone waiting to get a haircut. When Can napped in the afternoon, Kham would fill in for him. The first day, he wasn't used to it. Kham nicked a customer's ear, drew blood. This man got pissed off and instead of 70, only paid 30. Can used a pencil to jot down the daily intake in a notebook, a plus sign for 100, a circle for 200. Then he'd draw triangles with a dot in the middle for who knows what. Doai said: "Your accounting book is like espionage."

December 23 was *Mr.* Tao's Ascension Day. Sinh cooked bean threads, and everyone ate until their bellies were taut. Kham asked: "Why is he called *Mr.* Tao?" Doai said: "The story's like this: *Mr.* Tao stands for 'three hearthstones.' Once upon a time there were two brothers who married the same wife. She would sleep with one brother one night and the other brother the other night. The Jade King was moved by their close relationship and turned each one into a hearthstone so they could always be near each other. We call them Patron Saints of the Kitchen, or *Mr.* Tao." Sinh carried the tray into the kitchen. Kham said: "It was easy to become a saint in the old days." Old Kien said: "Don't listen to him." Doai said: "Then there is this other story. There was a daughter-in-law in this one household. The father-in-law grabbed her breasts. The son said: 'Why did you grab my wife's breasts?' The father said: 'To settle an old score. Why did you used to grab my wife's breasts?' It is said that these people also became saints." Can said: "Your stories, I don't get them." Old Kien said: "Don't listen to him."

On the 27th, Old Kien wrapped rice cakes. A vat and a half of sticky rice meant 28 cakes. There were two kinds of cakes, ones stuffed with peanuts and ones stuffed with sugar, the sugary kind were marked by a red string.

Sinh boiled the cakes. Doai hovered around the kitchen. Doai asked: "Do you know, Sinh, where the future of this house lies?" Sinh said: "No." Doai laughed: "Me." Sinh asked: "How's that?" Doai said: "Father's old. He'll die. Khiem will go to jail sooner or later. Kham, when he graduates, will be sent to either Tay Bac or Tay Nguyen. Ton we don't have to talk about. He's useless." Sinh asked: "Then what about Can?" Doai said: "That depends on you. If you love me, I can pick a fight with him and throw him out into the street." Sinh said: "As easy as that?" Doai said: "What are you hesitant about? Old Can is both stupid and cowardly and weak, the doctor said he's impotent. He's been married to you for two years now, and where are the children?" Sinh sat still. The pot of rice cakes boiled furiously.

Doai said: "I'll go into your room tonight, all right?"

Sinh grabbed the knife: "Go away. If you come near, I'll kill you!" Doai smiled wanly, pedaled backward and went into the house, muttering as he walked: "Women are evil."

On the 29th, Old Kien went to the market to buy a branch of peach flowers. On the evening of the 30th, Khiem bought home a large, potted mandarin orange tree, with three tiers of fruits, and a string of firecrackers measuring six meters. Kham said: "Getting extravagant here." Doai said: "He knows he has money." Kham said: "We two are known as educated, but come New Year's Day, we don't even have a decent suit to wear." Doai said: "The only way out is to marry a rich wife.

Tonight, you take me to the daughter of Mr. Daylight, all right?" Kham said: "Easy enough. If you can seduce her, what's my reward?" Doai said: "A watch." Kham said: "Good enough. You write down a few lines for me as proof." Doai asked: "Don't trust me?" Kham said: "No." Doai wrote on a piece of paper: "To sleep with My Trinh, the reward is a watch worth 3,000 *dong*. To marry My Trinh, the reward is 5 percent of the dowry. Day . . . month . . . year . . . Nguyen Si Doai." Kham put the scrap of paper into his pocket then said: "Thank you."

Kham said: "I heard Khiem telling that story yesterday, then I had a really scary dream last night." Doai asked: "What story?" Kham said: "Khiem talked about killing pigs. Two hands holding electric nodes to the temples of each pig. *Eech*, and it's over. During a power failure, Khiem had to use a sledgehammer to hit each pig on the back of the neck. With one strong pig, ten blows were not enough to kill him, his neck all messed up, Khiem, sleepy, hit the pig in the leg. During one shift, Khiem killed over a thousand pigs and was awarded a citation." Doai asked: "What about your dream?" Kham said: "I dreamt I had to kill a pig, one that wouldn't die, he only smiled at me, and as punishment, I was sent to clean up an entire cesspool. The cesspool was made of cement, measuring 10 x 6 x 1.5 meters, 90 square meters. A rainstorm came, flooding the cesspool, with me in it, shit in my mouth, in my ears." Doai said: "That's a good dream, you shouldn't worry about it. Buy a lottery ticket, you're sure to win. Old people say that stepping on shit means good luck. You were drowning in it, you'll probably hit the jackpot." Kham said: "Very true. If you hadn't told me I wouldn't have known." After saying that, he ran excitedly into town.

On New Year's Eve, there were only Khiem, Ton, and Sinh in the house. Hien's parents had sent their son down near dusk to invite Old Kien and Can to town. They were probably drunk and couldn't come home yet. Doai and Kham took My Trinh and My Lan to Ngoc Son Temple to pick flowers.

Khiem arranged a young hen Sinh had cooked earlier that evening on the altar, a rose in its beak. He also opened a box of jelly, poured three cups of wine, and laid out a pot of tea. Khiem said: "You handle the ceremony, Sister Sinh." Sinh put on a little lipstick, a pair of slacks, a long-sleeved sweater, an unbuttoned vest and a yellow scarf around the neck, and looked entirely different from her usual self. Sinh said: "You do it. I'm a woman, and know nothing about these kinds of ceremonies." Khiem said: "You're older, just bow three times and I'll take care of the prayer part." Sinh said: "Good enough." After saying that, she went in front of the altar, bowed three times, mumbled something, then bowed three more times. Not a person who's ignorant of ceremonial procedures.

Khiem said to Ton: "I hung the string of firecrackers near the door; after my prayer, you light it." After saying that, he stuck a lit filtered cigarette into Ton's mouth. Khiem said: "Light it with a cigarette like this." Ton nodded.

Khiem bowed three times, said: "The Socialist People's Republic of Vietnam, in the year . . ." Ton lit the firecrackers. Earth and sky became harmonious, human emotions stirred.

Khiem said: "It's a New Year, I wish you health and luck. Here's a thousand for good fortune." Sinh's eyes watered: "You're giving me this much? I also wish you a healthy New Year, five, ten times better than last year. Can keeps all the money, I have nothing to wish you luck with. Ton, take a hundred for luck, it's from Khiem." Ton held the bill up to the light, asked: "Money?" Khiem said: "Yes." Ton asked: "What's money?" Khiem said: "Money's king."

Old Kien and Can came home at 1 in the morning. A little later Doai and Kham also showed up. The whole house feasted until 3, closed their eyes for half an hour, got up again, cursorily bowed and prayed, then feasted some more. By 8, Old Kien said: "I'll go and visit the neighbors, Can and Sinh come with me. Khiem, give your father some money so he can wish people luck."

Old Kien and Can and his wife made the round. Old Kien

had on a pair of colonial work pants, a black shirt, and a black knitted cap. Can wore a major's uniform, bought at the flea market, with a hole in one sleeve from a cigarette burn. Sinh wore a pair of corduroy jeans and a German-made fur jacket. Kham said: "Sister Sinh looks like a queen."

Some neighbors dropped in. Doai came out to greet them. After wishing each other good luck, everybody sat down to drink tea and chatter. Doai said: "I'm sorry, Uncle, but I don't know how many people there are in your household or what their names are." The neighbor smiled: "Same here." Doai said: "In the old days, burglars had four categories of houses they wouldn't rob. The first was neighbors' houses, the second was friends' houses, the third was houses in mourning, and the fourth was houses in the middle of a celebration. I rob by the same set of rules and never break them." The neighbor smiled: "My sons are the same." After tea, everyone went home. The neighbor's son said: "That Doai is educated but talks a lot of trash." The neighbor said: "Chaos."

After three days of celebration, the streets were littered with spent firecrackers. Everyone felt that New Year's Day had passed too quickly! But which day doesn't pass too quickly, O God?

6. Night

By the end of March, Sinh's period stopped, she craved sour foods, retched every so often and her body stiffened: symptoms of pregnancy.

Old Kien got sick in May. Initially thought to be minor, it got worse gradually. At first, his eyesight only blurred, then he saw double, missing the door and walking into the wall. The whole house was worried and took him to the Western hospital. The doctor came up with a wild diagnosis of nerve disorder and prescribed B6. The doctor said: "Look here, these nerves are like this, when they clash, one becomes two, a chicken turns into a moor hen."

Can asked: "What is there to do, doctor?" The doctor said: "Medical science is investigating."

Bedridden at the hospital for a week, Old Kien's eyesight worsened. Doai said: "I suspect a wrong diagnosis." Doai went to someone he knew at the Eastern hospital. This man said: "Western medicine's nonsense. You can bring the old man here." Doai asked for a discharge for Old Kien. The doctor said: "Once you leave here, don't come back."

Old Kien stayed at the Eastern hospital, but didn't get any better, his body wasted away, his head hurt. By October, a brain tumor was detected. The doctor said: "If left like this he will die, but an operation may save him." Gathering the family for a meeting, Can said: "What to do? Since father's been sick, we've spent a lot of money." Can opened the account book and read from it: "Brother Khiem gave a thousand one time; 8,000 another time; 5,000 another time. Brother Doai gave a hundred one time, 60 another time; 1,100 another time. Brother Kham gave 300 one time, but when I gave him a thousand to buy medicines from Mr. Toai, the druggist, it only cost 500, the remaining 500 he kept and hasn't given back to me. Food cost is like this . . . like this . . . Who spent what I've written down."

Doai said: "I think he's too old, an operation won't change a thing, better to let him die." Ton sobbed out loud. Can asked: "What's your opinion, Kham?" Kham said: "Whatever you all decide, I'll go along." Can asked: "Why so silent, Khiem?" Khiem asked: "What have you decided?" Can said: "I'm thinking." Doai said: "What a waste of time. Who agrees that father should die raise your hand. I'll take the votes."

The day Old Kien had his brain operation everyone went to the hospital except Sinh and Ton. The procedure lasted forty-two minutes. Sitting in the waiting room, Doai said to Kham: "It's bad that the old man never wrote a will. How're we going to divide his assets later?" Kham said: "Old Can is so greedy, we will all end up on the streets." Doai said: "I'll marry My Trinh next year, Mr. Daylight has promised me one stick of gold. You think one stick's enough to buy a house?" Kham said: "In my hands, I can multiply it into several sticks." Doai said: "To have business skills is best, the other skills, like art, literature, etc., are all useless."

Can had a meeting with the doctor. Later, he walked out shaking his head: "The doctor said we can take father home in about a month."

The day Old Kien was taken home, his head was bandaged, he couldn't respond to questions, and his eyesight was bad. Inside the house, Sinh unwrapped his bandage. Old Kien's head was bald, with a lump the size of an egg. Half a month later, this lump increased to the size of a grapefruit, nudged with a finger it felt like there was bean paste inside, a big indentation for a big nudge, a little indentation for a little nudge. Sinh had to tend to the old man, a terrible job.

Kham asked Doai: "Is this illness contagious?" Doai said: "It's better to be careful. Can and his wife have money. Khiem has money. But if either one of us get sick, where do we get money for treatment?"

Soon after, Old Kien went into delirium, moaning always: "Please let me die. It hurts too much." The atmosphere in the house turned morbid, depressing everyone. Even Ton stopped washing the floor, all day long he'd sit by himself in the woodshed next to the toilet.

Mrs. Hien came down from the city, saw her brother writhing in pain and cried: "My brother, what debts haven't you paid to be tortured like this?" Mrs. Hien said: "You guys figure something out, or are you going to leave him like that?" Can asked: "What should we do?" Mrs. Hien said: "I have a friend who has a text of the Special Mantra, we can copy it and bring it back here to read, maybe then he'll go peacefully." Doai said: "Do it this evening."

Mrs. Hien made Khiem go to town, to this woman's house to copy the Special Mantra. Khiem brought it back and said to Doai: "You're good with words, you read it." Doai turned the piece of paper every which way and said: "I can't deal with your handwriting, it's worse than Can's accounting book."

Khiem read the mantra. It was dusk. Mrs. Hien lit incense and sat next to him. Old Kien was writhing at first, then lay still. At 11 o'clock, everyone went to bed. Khiem was still reading the mantra. Over and over. Basically the mantra asked Buddha to forgive the dying person's sins and to protect the ones left behind, in hard-to-understand language. Khiem read all night, his voice distorted. At 4 in the morning, Old Kien stopped breathing, a faint smile was on his lips, he looked very benign, serene. Khiem closed his father's eyes then went to tell Can. Everyone woke.

Doai said: "The old man's gone. How fortunate. I'll go buy a coffin."

7. A Normal Day

Forty days after Old Kien's funeral, Sinh gave birth to a baby girl. A party was planned to welcome her back from the hospital. Can and Kham went to the market. Khiem cooked. Doai and Ton cleaned up. The two girls, My Lan and My Trinh, came by, with flowers no less.

At the table, Sinh sat in the middle, with My Lan and My Trinh on either side. Sinh was radiantly beautiful. Doai poured wine into a cup, stood up and said: "This cup of wine I toast to life. This wine is both sweet and sour. Whoever accepts life then toast with me. Life is like a gust of foul wind but also very beautiful. To the newborn and to her future!" Everyone raised their cups. Doai said: "Hold on a second. But what's the baby's name?" Everyone laughed. Buoyant with wine, Khiem said: "Sister Sinh, is it rough being a daughter-in-law in the Si household?" Kham said: "Sister, you must say it in such a way as to not scare off My Lan and My Trinh." Sinh smiled: "If it's like this then it's not rough." Can asked: "Then it's rough normally?" Sinh said: "Of course it's rough. And very humiliating. A lot of pain and a lot of anguish. But

I also love it." Ton grinned and repeated innocently: "Also love it!"

The mailman passed the door and looked in: "Is this house numbered 29? There's a telegram." Can went out to accept it, then said: "Uncle Vy in Phuc Yen died at eight in the morning yesterday." Doai said: "We can deal with that later. What's so unusual about old people dying? Let's get on with this party. After you, Generals!"

Translated by Linh Dinh

THE RIVER'S CURSE

Tran Ngoc Tuan

*T*he protective spirit of our village worked with a bag and a cane, he was a beggar.

Each January, all the children in the village, rich or poor, went begging everywhere for about a month. It was also a way of paying homage to our ancestors.

I went back to my home village every year.

There, I could relive my early childhood and breathe in the pure air. My lungs were purged of the stench of the filthy city.

My father said: "Your vocation as a wordsmith is inferior to being a beggar."

My mother said: "Only when you go begging will you understand what's in man's heart. As for words, I just don't get it." (That's the logic of country folks; it's hard to explain words even to the enlightened.)

My village had the Luong River, a very benign river that flowed listlessly, like someone just waking up from sleep. Since when I don't know, but the villages on its opposite sides despised each other. In Vinh Village (our village), there were always confrontations involving both adults and children (just like in the days of the Trinh/Nguyen Lords).

In my village there were lucky families and accursed families. There were those who were successful, who passed exams to become government officials, bringing honors to the village, but also those who "sold their faces to the ground, their asses to the sky" their entire lives. Pitiful.

This I won't talk about any more because it's not unique to any one community; everywhere, there are tragicomic aspects to each individual fate. (This part I'll leave to the sociologists, the mediums, the astrologists, the sorcerers and card readers, those who tell fortunes by looking at chicken legs.)

1. Mrs. Indigent and Thoan

The village would only be an abstract place without actual people.

Mrs. Indigent was not an outsider but a native. Her husband served in the Colonial Army in France. She had three children, twelve grandchildren, and three daughters-in-law. Thoan, one of her grandchildren, was a playmate of mine from the time when we bathed together naked, before we knew what embarrassment was.

According to people in the village, Mrs Indigent was being punished by the river spirit. When young, she had bathed in the river during her period; drops of foul blood from her vagina had dripped into the river as the river spirit was throwing a feast. Humiliated in front of his guests, officials, generals, and subjects, the river spirit cursed: I'll punish her entire family; she alone will survive to mourn her relatives. This punishment was truly horrible (only someone very powerful could carry it out). Not satisfied, the river spirit also brought animosity to the two villages by the river (as I've said above).

Mrs. Indigent's three children (and her daughters-in-law) all drowned in succession in the benign Luong River, with its water flowing listlessly like someone just waking up from sleep. Every night, Mrs. Indigent went to the river to burn incense sticks and to leave fruit offerings, to beseech the river spirit to withdraw his punishment. In the dark night, she let her hair down; the embers from the incense sticks were as red as the eyes of a wolf, blurry, mysterious, occult. Her prayers were as follows:

> *Oh river spirit!*
> *Take your curse to the ocean*
> *So you can be more benevolent*
> *I had to cry for three children I gave birth to in pain*
> *Then I had to cry for three daughters-in-law*
> *All of them*
> *Died in your river*
> *Oh river spirit!*
> *If only because I had inadvertently*
> *Ruined your festivities*
> *Do you have to be angry for so long?*
> *Your mother also gave birth to you from blood*
> *Your mother also had periods*
> *That dripped into the river*
> *That I had to drink*
> *Flow rapidly river spirit*
> *Take your curse far away and don't come back*
> *Look and listen*
> *Be me for a minute*
> *Then you will pity me*
> *Oh river spirit*
> *Don't make my grandchildren die*
> *Please drown me*
> *In place of innocent people*

Thoan (Mrs. Indigent's granddaughter) and I often ran around in the fields. Her head was sunburnt, with innumerable head lice. We had a game we played with dog grass. If I lost, I had to catch twenty head lice. I would give each louse a sharp bite after catching it. The blood from the louse, or from Thoan (it was hard to tell), was always tasty, sweet, a bit salty.

My mother looked at Thoan and smacked her lips: "What a pity, so small and already an orphan, let me cure you of head lice." The next day, she took seeds from a custard apple, grinded them, mixed them with wine, rubbed them on Thoan's head, then covered her head with a towel. "Leave it alone for a day and a night." It was truly remarkable: there were no lice left on her head, not even eggs.

From then on, there was a new condition to the dog grass game. If I lost, I had to pull my pants down so Thoan could flick at my penis. I lost so many times once that my penis became all puffed up. Enraged, I tried hard to get even. When I won (which was seldom), I would pull Thoan's pants down and pinch her upper thigh, where the flesh was tender, so that she would shriek in pain. I would gloat like a victorious general, and scream in ecstasy the way a destitute man would in winning the lottery.

I often told her stories from long ago (the majority of which I made up). These stories generally ended with: "The poor suffering girl married the prince. She took money and gold and distributed them to the poor." Or: "The tiger roared, then ran into the forest." After hearing a story, Thoan said: "Back then, there were fairies and buddhas, and prayers were answered. Nowadays, when I pray, nothing happens."

I had seen, and heard, Thoan pray. It was very sorrowful and pitiable! She prayed like this:

> *Oh river!*
> *Don't make my grandmother kneel down each*
> *   night*
> *Our family is made up of human beings*
> *Like the shrimps and the fish, all children of the*
> *   river*
> *To appease you*

We have sacrificed six to the water
My grandmother's arms are worn out
From tying funeral headbands on our heads
The old leaf cries for the young leaves
Don't make our beloved ones leave in succession
Only to come back in death
Although we've erected a shrine
Loaded with sticky rice and meat offerings
The dead cannot eat it
Dead because of the river spirit
No one's a hero
In our family
There are ten death anniversaries a year
Oh river spirit!
I bow to you
Please be as magnanimous as your mother the sea
Oh river spirit!
Laugh and let go of your anger
Don't make our house
Be emptied of all occupants
Oh please river spirit!
Try to be kind
Don't hoard your anger
Strike your head on the ground
Be compassionate

After finishing middle school, I went to the district capital to continue my studies. Thoan stayed behind. When I went back home, we'd meet, but our relationship was not as carefree as before. Once, I asked Thoan to accompany me to town to see a stage performance. She wore a white blouse, black silk pants, her long hair braided and wrapped in a Chinese kerchief. She roasted corns to take along, and made me eat them. She said: "Corns in our village are sweet because of water from the Luong River." We watched a folk opera: a militiawoman had lost her entire family to an American bomb.

She used a rifle to shoot down the jet plane. The pilot parachuted down, and was now singing an aria (to the tune of "I'm About To Cross A Bridge") in the middle of the stage:

> *My name is An American Pilot*
> *American, eeee . . . riding a phantom bolt of thunder*
> *I was shot down, eeee . . . shot down into a rice*
> * paddy*
> *Now I beg everyone to forgive me . . .*

Thoan said: "Our folk opera is truly fantastic, considering. Even the American pilot knew how to sing."

At the end of the opera, the militiawoman had suppressed her grief and did not shoot the American. She tied him up and turned him in to the authorities. Thoan said: "Vietnamese are generous to outsiders, but mean-spirited to their own kind. Even now, Vinh Village and Quang Village are still feuding with each other."

It was as if I was paying no attention to my surroundings, but preoccupied only with chewing corns, tirelessly, the way a tiger chews pebbles.

Thoan died at eighteen.

My mother related: "Thoan's family buffalo tore away from its rope and jumped into the river. Thoan swam after it, past the sandbank (the demarcation between Vinh Village and Quang Village). The children in Quang Village tried to outdo each other throwing rocks. One probably hit Thoan in the head. The Luong River carried her away. Her corpse was only found three days later. Mrs. Indigent nearly passed out crying next to her granddaughter's corpse.

The flowing river had not lifted its curse . . .

It was moonless that night. I wandered along the river, under the faint light of a thousand fireflies. I looked at the surface of the river and imagined it to be the face of a terrible old man, laughing smugly and wickedly. A chilly wind wafting from the surface of the water gave me goose bumps.

Like a sleepwalker, I took mud and smeared it on my face. Near sunrise, I returned home. My mother asked: "Where did you go, Son, that you're looking so dazed?"

I answered: "I went to find what is lost. There is no comfort left, Mother."

My father said: "The lowlifes are the ones who are comforted. Gentlemen eat shit. It's better to be like Old Quan. Oblivious."

2. Old Quan

Old Quan was a migrant. No one knew where he was from originally.

Someone said that, way back, he was a mandarin, riding in cars, with servants. It made sense: he knew the Confucian classics, was fluent in history. He even knew French. Someone else said that Old Quan was a famous bandit leader, now lying low, incognito, his sword retired. That also made sense. I have seen Old Quan beat up, empty-handed, a whole gang of armed youths from Quang Village. That was the first time he showed what he was capable of, because the gang from Quang Village had swam across the river to steal sweet potatoes from our collective farm, and bloodied our militia guard's head.

Living alone, Old Quan fed himself by fishing and by planting vegetables. His house, at the end of the village, right at the foot of Chua Mountain, was forlorn, dismal, like an abandoned shrine.

Old Quan often asked me to pour rice gruel on banyan leaves to pray for those who died homeless and without relatives on Wandering Souls Day.

He confided: "There are spirits. I often talk to them. There's no need to be guarded, the dead never harm anyone. There is nothing, good or bad, they don't know about the living."

He counseled: "Before, people studied to improve themselves, to be righteous, to help others. Nowadays, people study only to gain notoriety. There are few who are truly exceptional. You should study the old ways."

I asked: "What is meant by helping others?"

He said: "If a king is enlightened, then he should become a mandarin after studying. But if a king is immoral, then he should hide in obscurity. If everyone is good, then it is bad to be impoverished. But if everyone is base, then it is disgraceful to be among the privileged."

I flashed my teeth: "A mandarin's famous enough. Who needs a king?"

He said: "If a mandarin is famous, maybe he's a phony, pretending to be righteous. You look closely, and he's only one of those who knows how to 'dig into walls.'"

I said: "It's hard to tell them apart. I think all mandarins are equally impressive."

He laughed: "A man knows himself. Shit inside the belly will come out sooner or later. You can't hide it."

I boldly asked: "Way back, you were a mandarin, right? Or a bandit leader?"

He laughed again (as gentle as a buffalo calf): "Mandarins and head bandits are not different from each other. They differ only in their means, and what they are called."

I answered: "It's much more impressive to be a bandit leader. You're the big shot of an entire region."

He shouted: "Nonsense! A self-destructive errant knight wandering in the woods is still considered by most people to be a hoodlum."

Old Quan often cooked rats for me to eat. Fussily prepared, it took up a whole day. The rats he caught were often the plump ones, from the rice paddies. I got impatient just watching him boil water to pluck the hair. The water could not be boiled for too long; little bubbles were just popping on the surface. Old Quan said: "The best part of a rat is the skin, which overheated water would ruin. Dip the rat into the water, pluck it clean, and remember to cut out the bladder, liver, and testicles, else it would stink, even a dog won't eat it. After pulling the rat from the water, you have to rub it with salt, then you get rid of the head, the intestines, and the feet. Boil the water once more, leave the rat inside the pot, uncovered. When the broth is clear, pull the rat out. Chop some lime leaves. Dip the meat in fish sauce with hot peppers and garlic. There is also the roasted dish. I'll let you enjoy it some other time."

Enjoying rat meat and wine, he banged his chopsticks and sang hoarsely. The lyrics sounded mournful but were extremely arrogant:

> *The sky's nothing*
> *The earth's the same*
> *I'm only a guest here*
> *Glory's a dream*
> *I'm a solitary man*
> *Women are like roses*
> *Flowers with thorns*
> *Cowards fear thorns*
> *So as to be in charge*
> *I'll hack it with a sword*
> *I'll be a loner my whole life*
> *I throw up love onto a straw mat*
> *I can't digest a single female*
> *I shit on all celestial beings*
> *And on all the royal tombs*
> *I'm the only man*
> *Everyone wears a mask*
> *But everyone's a wolf*
> *I curse the one who gave birth to me*
> *My misshapen self*
> *Was made from my parents' obscenity*
> *La . . . La . . . La . . .*
> *In my soul*
> *Is the river's curse*
> *Against a barbaric yellow race*

My skin's also yellow
The punishment is solitary confinement
But I'm not alone
My friends are the ghosts
My lovers are the demons
I'll rape the sun
I'll kidnap the moon for ransom
I'll use the stars as seasoning
To marinate rat meat
I'm still me
Dead broke, with a lavish soul
I'm a solitary
With neither family nor possessions
Oh river!
Your curse has caused many conflicts
Only poetry can erase hatred
It's a shame I'm not a poet
To nullify your curse
Don't make these lowlifes
Die in fear of offending others
You don't know folk poetry
You can't even speak proper Vietnamese
Don't make us downtrodden
Speak the language of the white skin with yellow
  hair
Or the red skin with black eyes
This entire tribe was hatched from a sack of eggs
La, la, la . . . Oh, melon . . .
I'm still me.

Done with singing, Old Quan was inspired enough to skip out to the courtyard to show off his martial arts.

With flickering movements, his feet raked the earth, creating grooved patterns. Only the whistling air could be heard. After the snake routine, he started on a homage to the ancestors' kata. The source of his style was hard to place.

It was a patchwork, sly, wicked, clearly a martial art of forest bandits. He thrust his hand into the trunk of a banana tree, spun and kicked a water jar to bits, then innocently head-butted a rotting wall, collapsing it.

He asked me: "You like to study martial arts?"

I answered: "I'm a little guy. I wouldn't dare."

He said: "It doesn't matter if you're little. Suppleness will overcome strength. A silk rope could tie up an elephant."

I said: "If you have to resort to martial arts, then you're a coward."

He said: "It's true! Force is clueless. Try hard to learn words."

Old Quan was looking for death, or maybe death was looking for him, it was hard to tell. My father told me: "That year, the Luong River's water level rose (it happens only once every fifty years). Old Quan was drunk, he drowned inside his own house."

The river's curse does not spare even a migrant.

3. Conclusion

After reading this story, my wife (who is knowledgeable about literature and is working for a magazine in the capital) said:

"According to you, how many characters are there in this story?"

I said: "Three."

She said: "No, four, including the river. You should revise the poetry parts, the prayers, and the songs sung by the characters. Get rid of what Thoan said after watching the folk opera, generally 'forgiving to outsiders.' We are practicing diplomacy out of self-interest. It's not fitting to write that."

After contributing those opinions, my wife stopped talking. The associate head editor came by to pick her up, as usual. He greeted me gushingly . . . That night, I saw Thoan clearly in a dream. She was walking on water, wearing pristine, white clothing. She said to me: "You should burn my prayer, then mix it with the blood of one devoid of anger. Only then will the river's curse be nullified."

I woke up suddenly. My wife, lying next to me, was mumbling: "Deeper and harder, Q, I'm climaxing, faster."

I spat in her face (it turned out she'd been planting horns on my head). Q was the name of the associate head editor at the magazine where my wife was working.

The next morning, I went back to my home village. That night, feeling impotent, I went to the river and cried. Where would I find the blood of one devoid of anger? (Maybe only a monk could fit that requirement.) But how would I ask for blood from one? I did not want to be a murderer. Forgive me, Thoan! The river's curse was certainly severe.

I sobbed when I realized that I was like a floating duckweed on the surface of the river, helpless against the flow of destiny.

The Luong River flowed on. It looked at me as if in mockery.

Translated by Linh Dinh

SCENES FROM AN ALLEY

Le Minh Khue

$\mathcal{O}$n the past, honest people rarely dared to enter this dark and stinking alley at night. In those days, the alley had no electricity. It was a place where people dumped their trash and where squatters built huts out of stray pieces of wood and sacks of rice, establishing a neighborhood of creeps. Over the past two or three years, it seemed like this alleyway suddenly awoke from its ignorant sleep. It came alive, full of houses with trees and plants. The faces there were also transformed. They were human now, no longer as beastly as before.

In the depths of the alley lay Quyt's two-story house. In the past, Quyt's father had received the death penalty for murdering somebody. Instead of remarrying, his mother picked trash to raise her child. By bribing someone, she arranged for Quyt to go work as a laborer in the Great Nation of Germany. Five years later, he returned and transformed their miserable hut into a two-story villa. Western currency could perform magic more powerful than a fairy's. If you wanted a multi-story house, it would instantly materialize. If you wanted a guard dog or ornamental plants, they'd be yours in the blink of an eye. And you could even have a wife who was as beautiful as a dream, a real intellectual and fluent in English. Every day, Quyt and his wife came and went like a prince and princess. They had a son who inherited all of the traits of his father: a pouting lip, eyes like slits, crooked nose, and stunted limbs. But he always dressed in the most fashionable clothes and he always wore foreign cologne, so he wasn't such an eyesore.

The couple and their son slept on the ground floor. The second floor was very spacious, and they rented it out to a Westerner who was as big as a steamroller. The Western guy did some kind of work for a foreign company in the center of town. He was seen driving his own car, and every morning he could be heard breathing laboriously through his exercises in the alleyway, showing a body that was as hairy as a gibbon's. Every night he came home late, smelling of alcohol, and every night he brought a prostitute up his private stairway. It was said that Quyt and his wife even got something on top of the rent for allowing that. Money makes money, as the saying goes.

Before Quyt went away to work as a laborer in Germany, there was never a time when his house wasn't full of the sound of quarreling. Now there was only sweet talk. As for their son, Quyt's wife complained to the neighbors that although the house was always full of such delicacies as pork sausage, fresh milk, and imported apples and pears, the boy would never touch them. She dressed like a queen, worked for a foreign company, and sometimes you could see her laughing until her eyes puckered up, saying, "Well! Well!" in English to the Western guy who rented their house.

That guy was a nasty drinker. Every time he came home at night, he revved the engine at the top of the alley and raced on in. It would be disastrous for anyone who was too slow to get out of his way. For some time, people had been afraid, and by 10 o'clock at night they'd be in a state of suspense, not daring to show their faces in the street. When they heard the sound of his car from far away, the old people would plug their ears and crawl under their blankets. Even on nights when the car didn't make a lot of noise, when he was only slightly drunk, people still knew that there was a woman in the car. They'd learned his ways. It wasn't until the last day of the month, when he was at his drunkest, that he would be alone. That was the time that his money was running short and he could only afford alcohol and nothing else. Once he'd gotten to his room, he'd go out onto the balcony and sing at the top of his lungs. Hearing him even from far away, children would huddle closer to their mothers, and dogs would race to their gates and howl. The whole neighborhood was in an uproar.

Two alleys away from Quyt's house lay the home of a gentleman who'd just been promoted to a big position in one of the city's more important companies. His given name was To and when he was young he and his mother had picked trash in this neighborhood. Thanks to his hardworking mother, To was able to make it to high school. He became a soldier in April of '75, a convenient time to enter the army because that was the month the war ended and many people had died already. He was sent to a city in central Vietnam as part of its military government and took on the responsibility of weeding the place of capitalists. When he returned to the north, he looked like a person who had made so much money he had no need of making any more. The company where he worked found him very conscientious, so they promoted him to the top rank. Once he had established his career, he dropped his peasant's name in favor of something more refined. Now he called himself Toan. He had a secretary and whenever they rode in a car together, he would get out first and open the door for her. He entertained his customers with Western whiskey. But even though he'd attained a high position and a great deal of wealth, he was uncultured. After work he would order the chauffeur to drive straight to a club. He was crazy about massage and he like to hold the tender thighs of the young women sitting on his lap in this dark and dreamy atmosphere. All of his colleagues liked that as well. With a woman on either leg, the men would wrap their arms around the women's waists, open their mouths and wait to be fed like babies. This was an unusual form of enjoyment that men in our country loved.

For some months it had been known that he kept a mistress, which met the last remaining requirement of a peasant who had risen to a high rank. He had bought her a house and whenever he wanted entertainment he could go there. In order to maintain her husband's reputation, his cunning wife never picked a fight in public, but in secret she often bit him. One day there was a welt as big as a guava on his forehead. He tried to explain it by saying that the stairs in his house were too slippery.

Toan's poor father was over ninety years old. Although he was both deaf and a slow walker, he still had a good appetite. All day long, the old man would perk up whenever he saw anyone's lips moving. He loved to sit and watch, just like a baby who hadn't learned to turn over yet. Maybe it was because of him that Toan didn't dare pick a fight with his wife. At any rate, the daughter-in-law was still willing to wash the old man's hands and feet, blow on his rice to cool it down, and cook him bowls of vegetable broth. He would have had to wait forever for his son to do that. The son was always in a meeting. After work, it would be massage and beer and women.

"Damn the man born in obscurity, with his feet buried deep in the water of the fields. Now that he has money, he drools after everything and imitates other people just like a monkey." The wife would curse at random, and the deaf old father-in-law would prick up his ears like a donkey.

Sometimes, his uppity son would look at him with rage, thinking, "Why don't you hurry up and die?"

* * *

One evening, the Western guy renting Quyt's house got completely drunk. He drove his car home earlier than usual.

When the car entered the head of the alley, he ran into

something and hit the brake in panic. He sobered up immediately. The residents of the alley rushed outside, and in an instant there was a crowd. Whose child is it? She was dead already. Pick her up! What a tragedy.

The car had run over her head. Her broken neck tilted to one side and her blood streamed into the street. It was Miss Ti Cam—Little Mute—the daughter of Mrs. Tit. The two of them had come here together, no one knew where from. People would only see them build a fire at night to cook some rice under the *sau* tree at the head of the lane. Miss Ti Cam, who was both mute and rather crazy, would sit idly waiting for her mother. Mrs. Tit went scavenging and she would wash out the pieces of plastic she'd found and lay them to dry on the sidewalk. She also collected empty cans and bought scrap metal. In short, she did anything in order to raise her daughter.

Being both mute and rather crazy, one day Miss Ti Cam found her way to the train station where a gang of rough young men dragged her into a back corner. There she lay quietly while they molested her. Passersby felt their hair standing on end when they heard the hoarse laughter of the beasts mixed with the grunts of Miss Ti Cam, who sounded like a bitch in heat. The noise coming from behind the station, the noise of sin and the noises of the night enveloped the sobs of poor Miss Ti Cam. Over the past three months, her stomach had grown, bringing Mrs. Tit to the verge of tears. Pregnant, Miss Ti Cam seemed a little less crazy, and she no longer went back and forth smiling to herself. Instead, she sat listlessly at the base of the tree. Several times, a charitable organization had brought a car around to pick them up and take them to its headquarters so that the government could care for them, but after a few days they always found their way back. They were like wild grasses accustomed to living in a field. How could they bear to live in a cage?

Mrs. Tit threw herself across the body of Miss Ti Cam. "Oh my child, I brought you into this miserable life and now you have to die like this!"

Toan and his wife came out to the spot to see what had

happened. Toan's expression was very strange. Something like the flash of a great discovery appeared to cross his face and he brightened up for a moment.

Quyt and his wife looked terrified. They would probably lose their renter because of this. After this incident would the Western guy dare to stay? If he wanted to stay, he would have to spend a fortune on bribery.

The body of Miss Ti Cam was still warm and dozens of people were already thinking of profits and losses. The whole neighborhood was as noisy as a broken beehive, and the Westerner was flailing his arms, shrugging his shoulders, and screeching like an ancient record player with a dull needle. His breath still smelled of alcohol.

Within a few days, people had figured out how much fault to attribute to the victim and how much fault to attribute to the driver. As it turned out, Miss Ti Cam had thrown herself under the Westerner's car. As for him, he had been drunk and therefore had not been able to apply the brakes in time. Otherwise, he hadn't broken any rules. Because of that he wasn't indicted, but he still had to pay Mrs. Tit damages amounting to 10 million *dong* (U.S. $1,000) on top of the funeral expenses.

After burying her child, Mrs. Tit was walking on clouds because, all of a sudden, she had 10 million *dong* in her hands. It was said that the Westerner also gave her a gold chain that weighed three-tenths of a tael. In the space of an instant, Mrs. Tit had become a millionaire. She immediately bought herself a place in the alleyway, built a kitchen and then remodeled it, all of which cost three million. She didn't deal in scrap metal anymore. She bought a small glass cabinet and brought it home to display sundries for sale. She was just over fifty years old and she had money, a shop and a gold chain weighing three-tenths of a tael around her neck. It was still a peasant's neck, but now it was also a wealthy one, so a few men often parked their scooters in front of her glass cabinet in order to chat with her. Who knows, perhaps in the near future she'd be riding in a bridal car. The neighbors were already huddling together gossiping about her, the same woman they once spit on whenever she and her daughter accidentally made too much smoke when they were cooking something under the tree. Mrs. Tit herself had been transformed. She spoke more gently, used fewer obscenities, and one day she bought herself a flowered hat.

Toan and his wife didn't tell each other what they were thinking, but both were obsessed with the same idea whenever they looked at the old deaf man sitting in the rattan chair reserved for him. Summer had arrived. People in the neighborhood often pulled chairs outside to catch the breezes. During these days, Toan and his wife made a show of their love for the old man. One could see them carrying out the chair with him in it and setting it down by the front door. Often, the old man was already fast asleep. There were times when Toan's wife forgot him when she turned on the electric fan inside the house and fell asleep. Sometimes it was nearly midnight before she'd remember the old man in the chair outside.

During this time, Toan's business was prospering. His company was doing so well that he hired an extra secretary to help him. She often wore miniskirts and was unlike the first secretary, who was reserved and came from a good family. If Toan was dozing off in the director's office in the afternoon, this new secretary often came up behind him, put her hand on his forehead and pressed her breast into his back. Her hands were so cool that his heart almost stopped beating, and the sound of her whispering in his ear made him melt like water. He thought gloomily of his children and also of his wife, who often fondled him quietly in a corner of the kitchen. But he couldn't leave his wife because he needed her. He needed her as a nurse for his old deaf father, who seemed unwilling to die anytime soon. Oh, this horrible fate of his.

Every night, both the husband and wife thought about Mrs. Tit. They wished they could be like her, finally rid of their terrible burden, while at the same time suddenly finding themselves with some extra millions in their pockets. This family was rich already. But who would turn down a few million more? If luck came their way and the drunk Westerner happened to plow into their ninety-year-old father, they wouldn't accept only 10 million. No, it would have to be more. Double that. Westerners were very rich. Anyway, the most important thing was to have a legal way to rid the family roster of the old man's name. To think that a beautiful house like theirs was dirtied by an old man's stinking urine! How could their fate be so horrible?!

Whenever their obsession reached such a point, although neither husband nor wife said a word to the other, they both pricked up their ears. It was still summer, and only in summer could they use the pretext of the cool breezes to let a ninety-year-old man fall asleep outside. But why during these days was the Westerner so rarely drunk? He no longer sped into the alley, but instead drove very slowly. Surely, though, one day he would forget the past and drive like he used to, like he had on the night he ran over Miss Ti Cam!

The husband and wife looked at each other, breathless because they had the same idea, but neither dared to tell the other.

* * *

Deep inside the alley, Quyt's house was located behind a fence covered by creeping vines, and the light in the Westerner's window still burned brightly. Quyt's wife was speaking English with the Westerner, caressing him and warning him not to drive recklessly into the alley as he had in the past. The Westerner said "okay" many times and did not forget to kiss the hand of Quyt's wife, his thick lips lingering on the ruby ring she wore on her little finger.

Quyt was more devoted than ever to the Westerner who rented his house. He brought prostitutes home for the renter. He brought alcohol home for him. There was also the night that Quyt's wife even disappeared from his bed, and he just ignored it—as long as the Westerner continued to rent the house. As long as he forgot the past incident and as long as the bribes he paid still had their effect. Oh, a blue-eyed, long-nosed man was a gold mine.

And every midnight, Toan and his wife came out and carried the rattan chair with the old man in it back into the house. It wouldn't look good if they let him sleep there all night.

* * *

One night, the alley was already nearly empty by 9 o'clock. There had been heavy winds in the late afternoon but it hadn't rained. The cool air had sent people to bed early. Toan's father was sitting outside in the rattan chair, just like any other night. He was breathing softly, like a child. Suddenly, an uproar started among a group of gamblers squatting next to Mrs. Tit's house. Two punks argued with each other, and one chased the other down the alley. One of them ran like an arrow. The other followed him, screaming, "Your mother's fart, I'll break your head open!"

He hurled the brick in his hand at his rival. It arced toward the ground, ricocheted off the base of the tree, and flew against the head of the sleeping ninety-year-old man. The two punks vanished.

The old man was strong and so he wasn't badly hurt. He only fainted. Toan and his wife carried him into the house and from that day on he was bedridden. He ate well but couldn't make it to the toilet.

The doctor came to examine the patient and told the daughter-in-law, "He can't walk yet, but he's still strong. If you take good care of him, he may even live to be a hundred!"

Toan and his wife looked at each other in dismay. Suddenly both of them cursed the Westerner. Damn him! Why had he been driving so carefully? How could things have come to this?

Translated by Bac Hoai Tran and Dana Sachs

THE WAY STATION

Do Phuoc Tien

O wandered for a long time through the coastal provinces. My pointy skull got even longer. Like a long, faded ear of corn. With the cross-eyed guy from Chao Zhou, I hunted antiquated clocks on the walls and tables, I gathered old eyeglass frames, gas cans from the fishing boats, helicopter metal. In short, I lived off scrap metal. For example, the bulky hooks from the cranes on the agricultural construction sites, or the steel chains that could chain up a tractor. My business didn't go too well. Mainly because in a tropical climate the rain and the sun come and go without any warning. One day, our pockets were empty. Stunned, we had to look reality in the face: we were both scrawny, lazy men. We never did have much luck. If luck would have been of any use in the scrap metal trade.

The Chao Zhou was as scrawny as a wisp of straw, unstable, shifty, terribly stingy. He dragged a huge clock around with him. It was his loudspeaker, his talisman.

Unhappiness made us vindictive, quarrelsome, morose. My companion spent the days laughing maniacally. That monstrous, ridiculous clock reverberated miserably through the slums, the back alleys. Tumbling in the wind, it echoed over the deserted rooftops, spreading its surreal cries of hunger and thirst, calling to us all those who had scrap metal to trade. Then one day we were destitute. We collapsed on the side of a cesspool where they raised catfish. Panting, convulsed with hunger, we dreamt of a sweet-and-sour soup full of *giac* fruit. An enormous soup. Our stomachs turned. It suddenly became clear: our baseness, our regrets, our fear of the future. Time passed.

The Chao Zhou got to his feet first. He pulled together his failing strength. He said that in spite of it all he and I were men, that a dream soup couldn't nourish a great ambition, that our nightmare of wandering had to end right here, on the edge of a catfish cesspool, that our salvation wouldn't come like tropical rains, that heaven would never provide for us, that you had to hunt it down, like you hunted a woman, had to seize the moment, bite into it, even if it meant taking from the pockets of others. And that . . . and that . . . hundreds of "thats"; they all stank of dried gudgeon fish, of coconut cake. I listened, listless. A deep weariness. I felt my body disintegrate, my will dissolve.

Spring came. In desperation we separated. I left for the North, fleeing the salt marshes, the mauve-colored dusks that haunted my vagabond dreams. The Chao Zhou left for the far South. And that was how we began our plan.

The home of Liem the Chinese was easy to find. A dazzling gate lacquered red. Rising around it, a hedge of longan and bilinga trees. Already, it was sinking into decrepitude. Walls whitewashed with lime. The roof, with its alternating male and female tiles, gaped open. Toward the back, the building looked like a real rat trap. An old wooden staircase led to the first floor. A fireplace stood out like an old broom. The whole place had something sinister, unsettling about it. The city lay under a constant swirl of dust. Desperate, silent, dismal little taverns lined the narrow back alleys.

According to the plan, I was to work for the Chinese for two years, the time needed to get back on my feet. I had to do a bit of everything: taste the wine, stuff Chinese sausages, marinate the chicken in herbs, make the "thousand-year-old" pickled eggs and, if I was lucky, still have time left to ponder the art of making sweet-and-sour noodles with ten different kinds of meat or steamed carp. If one day I could master the art of fondue in satay sauce, his entire culinary empire would fall into my hands. Don't forget, this was the kitchen of a restaurant owner from Ha Mon. This was the solution that the Chao Zhou and I had agreed on.

To be honest, I'm good for nothing. But for several seasons now I've worked like an ox, and I'm just clever enough to understand that I'm going to have to work even harder if I don't want to be squashed like an ordinary cockroach. Like everyone else, I have the right to eat my fill, sleep peacefully, maybe even escape my loneliness.

I really liked the Khmer, a pensive, generous man who was as dark and fat as a field rat. When you are in the same wretched situation, share the same fate, you accept each other easily, fall quickly into solidarity—at least that's what I think. Our friendship was sealed thanks to a cigarette lighter that snapped when you opened it. The Khmer liked it a lot, even though it clashed with his rubber tobacco pouch. At night, while I hid in a corner to eat the pork spareribs I had stolen the night before, the Khmer, a sarong rolled over his stomach, would quietly roll a cigarette in front of the oven. He had worked for Liem the Chinese for a long time, a very long time, maybe even before my miserable self came into the world. All you had to do was watch the way he butchered the animals to be sure of it. He slaughtered like one of the Binh Xuyen gang: His knife ripped the stomach toward the throat, slightly to the left. In general, Khmers don't like to change their profession or place of residence. Like tropical plants, they wilt when they are uprooted.

The Khmer's workload was terribly heavy. Each week, on top of his regular job, he had to kill two or three goats. Sometimes four if the restaurant was going well. They bought kid goats and fattened them tenderly, carefully, until their coats shone like sesbania sprouts at the end of winter. Then we force-fed them a strong cane-sugar alcohol, attached empty tin cans to their tails and chased them through the town until they collapsed from exhaustion. They expired quickly under the Khmer's expert blade, next to his sweaty body, his haggard, languid gaze.

The restaurant was open all day. But it was late at night, after the tornadoes of dust had subsided, that it really bloomed.

Another man lived there: he was the guest of honor. A swatch of flowered fabric wrapped around his hip, he swept the terrace with a jet of water and then, with an innate dignity, set the tables. A corpulent Indian placed a two-handled pot on the hearth, with an indifferent, contemptuous air. The Khmer salted the smoked goat quarters. Me, I mashed the meat with a noisy grinder. By the time they lit the gas lamp, the Chinese was slightly drunk. A glass of wine mixed with soda in his hand, he chuckled jovially with his guests, evaluating each dish we served with the eye of an inquisitor. The Chinese had his own work. He reserved certain tasks for himself, forbidding us to do them. For example: Hanging the lamps, serving wine, cashing money, and making change were all part of his exclusive domain.

The Indian always finished first. While we cleaned up, he would retire to a corner and drone interminable, monotonous prayers in front of a tiny oil lamp. His squat body slumped over as he entered deeper into dialogue with the Spirit.

Once I had piled up my ten piles of sawdust, I would find a way to go see Chu. She lived on the first floor. There I could relax a bit, savor the peace of the soul as if I were in my own home (that is, if ever I were fated to have one). Chu was there, day in and day out, seated in the middle of a pile of plastic roosters that sang when they jumped on their springs. The Chinese had declared the first floor off limits to everyone except the maid, Hoa. I entered through a skylight on the roof, tense, feverish, I would approach Chu. I knew that I was not the only one. One morning, I saw the Chinese come down first and go straight to the fountain. The Khmer was rinsing the earthenware pots used to mix wine and goat's blood. The Chinese drew near, pressing his face up against the Khmer's neck. They stared each other down for a long time. The Chinese pulled out the lighter that clicked when it opened, looked at it for a moment and then placed it on top of an earthenware jar next to the Khmer. He left without a word.

Chu told me that ever since she could sit up she had lived up there in that wooden cage. She told me that she would stay there until the room collapsed, until it crumbled under the piles of sawdust that rose up from below. I didn't believe her. For lunch I ate the cakes she put aside for me, just to pacify her, lull her into thinking of me as a harmless child. I massaged her tired, decrepit muscles. I listened to her talk on nights bathed in the silvery light of the full moon; she would search the clouds that drifted over the rooftop. And she forced me to rap in cadence with the passage of time, the time that hurtled through the male and female tiles, that darted through the dark, twisting alleys. Life down there was violent, wrapped in its trance; even the Chinese himself didn't belong to her world. She was half-paralyzed, one leg and an arm were useless.

The Chinese treated us well. I never doubted my boss's generosity. I understood and admired the tenacity, the will, the pride of the men from Xiamen, and more generally, of the Chinese, who had struggled to restore dignity to their race. All Liem the Chinese had was Chu. There was no question that he suffered. The alcohol in soda could only soften the bitter pain that weighed on him. It was, at best, a temporary tranquilizer. And the Chinese proved himself worthy of his race; he endured the shame of Chu's existence with an extraordinary stoicism. He would praise to the skies the withered celery or the shriveled mushrooms we brought him from distant villages cracking under the drought. He was a good small businessman, but that was all. He didn't dare choose, couldn't imagine another way out, another way to assert himself in the world. I was his complement: the girl, Chu, was a key objective in our plan.

Day by day, I devoted more and more time to Chu. More and more energy as well. When she sank into despair, I drew on all the tricks I had learned as a street hawker. I hate tears, I hate silence. Chu's tears trickled slowly. It took a whole night for them to barely reach her chin. Her tears reminded me of the wretchedness of my life. So I hugged her in my arms. And I imitated the Chao Zhou. I would tell her that . . . that the clouds were lost vapors risen from the waters, stupid, cowardly on top of it, deeply cowardly because they let the wind decide their fate, because they gave it time to shred their frail, impotent bodies. I would tell her that time is nothing, nothing but a hollow drum that beats against itself, that the traveling dyer perhaps doesn't live a life superior to mine, to hers . . . that time is only an idiotic, organic movement of sensations, that it had no basis, that nothing was of any consequence . . . that she or I, or anyone in this world, we are only a plow plodding through time, that our desires are only rusty anchors that chain us to humanity, that to be trapped in this life, like her, or to wander until death, like me, came to the same thing, that only inner accomplishment could open a road to a human world.

Our little comedy lasted a year. I couldn't continue anymore after that; I didn't have the strength. When I had concocted this plan with the Chao Zhou, I had never imagined this outcome. When I held her body in my arms, I actually thought about goodness, about real goodness. That was how it happened. Even the rotten scrap metal I had once dragged around had a value that somehow defied the laws of exchange. Chu was like that. My head nestled in her warm, tender bosom, I glimpsed, terrified, in this decomposing body, an infinite yearning; the desire to be human; the sincere, transparent, tumultuous desire of two passionate beings. The soul, if it exists, has nothing to do with its rather seedy lodging. Straightaway I came to a conclusion: Absolute freedom is just a decadent desire; it brazenly accepts all infidelities. I strained to manage my love gently, contrary to the ruthless illusions I had had. But always, like a child, I was obsessed with the idea that before me, in this bed, other wild storms had passed. That I was just a puppet who filled the pause between two tempests. With my taut muscles, my stubborn silence. And I imagined how the Khmer ravished Chu, how he would do it with his resolute, meticulous gestures, as if he were butchering a goat. In the grip of such paranoia, what could I do? In my arms as well, Chu expired quickly, her body panting with sweat, her breasts blushing with pleasure.

Of course I loved her, but of course, not for a single instant did I lose sight of my goal: To make a fortune. I suffered for having to continue this weary life in the shadow of the Chinese. The wooden cage with its stale odor of pickled turnips haunted me, even in my sleep. I often imitated the Chinese, drinking to chase away the dark premonitions in my brain. Of course, this bitter alcohol stung my tongue; this too I had stolen. But like I say, alcohol is only a mediocre, impotent tranquilizer compared to the terminal agony of being human. It is the shame of who we are that gives us the strength to pull ourselves up, but it also holds the temptation to put an end to it all. True or false, only experience will decide, but a premonition doesn't wait.

Then a day came, a very green spring day. I was coming back from the train station, dragging a cart filled with sawdust. The March wind tumbled through the streets in gusts, filling my mouth with a dry, salty dust. The gate was wide open. The paved courtyard was deserted. On the verandah, the old Indian gazed, distraught, at his oil lamp, contemplating the flies as they basked in the sun. From behind, somewhere in the air, coming from the mousetrap on the first floor, the sound of crying. Exhausted from fatigue and the sun, reeling, heavy with a premonition of disaster, I mounted the staircase. It was deserted. I couldn't believe it. A voice sobbed softly. Had my worst fears come true? And yet, it was certain, yesterday evening, from the same staircase, I had seen the Chinese and the Khmer quarreling. The Chinese was no ordinary man, that much I knew. I saw shadows gesticulating on the first floor and ran up. On the last step, I stopped, paralyzed.

On the bed where night after night we had fraudulently loved each other, there were two people. In my place (or that of the Khmer, it's all the same), was the maid, Hoa. Chu lay sprawled on her back, her mouth ajar, her eyes open wide, horrible. Sobbing, the maid gripped Chu's body, curling up against her like a shrimp. An unfinished meal lay on the table next to the bed. Overturned bowls. Rice scattered on the floor. A broken chopstick embedded in the mat. The sobs didn't come from Hoa's trembling shoulders. They seemed to rain down from the worm-eaten roof.

The guest of honor stood under the skylight. His neck tilted rigidly to one side to support his dignified head, as if it might collapse under the emotion. The Khmer stood pressed up against the wall, his sullen face aflame. The Chinese was seated in the only chair in the room. He was rigid, pale, like the plastic roosters strewn on the floor. There was no sawdust in the air. But the room seemed ready to crumble under the hatred of their looks, the mute violence of their breathing, the oppressive fury of men.

I watched, as if through a turbulent dream, the Khmer take a bowl of soup. He pours a bit of bouillon into his palm, spreads it out, sniffs it. He hesitates, like a field rat before poisoned bait. He stares fixedly at the railing, where the fine crosshatching of the wood etches shadowy designs. There, perhaps, night after night, was the place Chu had trysts with the clouds of her dreams. For a long time I felt their movements in the cracking of my brain. I saw the Khmer approach the chair, the bowl of soup in his hand. Calmly, gently, simply, he dumped it over the Chinese's head. A celery leaf dripped slowly down the forehead onto the cheekbone, down his chin, slipping onto his thigh. The Chinese sat motionless, his hands clutching the arms of the chair. The soup trickled, yellow and murky, down his face. Briskly, the Khmer wiped his hands. And then he left. He never came back.

I collapsed on the floor. The traveling dyer's drum, with its warlike charges, hammered on my skull. And time passed. Frozen, empty time. Listen, Chu, do you hear, for the first time, the rhythmic time of your first steps. My illusions had been shattered.

A few days after Chu's funeral, the Indian left. The spring hadn't had time to fade. Flies basked in the sun, obscene, plunged languidly into the oil of the old lamp, wriggled, and died. The Indian left with a shrug. The Spirit had shamelessly killed his faith. He left without a word, forgetting to pay for the oil that the Chinese had always supplied him with. I stayed on a bit longer. I had no ambition, no plans. Cooking no longer appealed to me. There was no possession I dreamed of having. I had loved Chu. It was difficult for me to distance myself from that room, where the nights of the full moon resonated with memories like long howls. The guest of honor also finally left. The Chinese couldn't keep him any longer. The alliances that he had painstakingly woven had unraveled in his hands.

In the end, they threw me out the red gate with the goat bones. Collapsed on the roadside like a dog, I gnawed my thoughts. I don't regret those months, the years that I lived like a rat caught in a trap. I knew that we couldn't live for long together, with those who live behind the tall hedgerows.

I thought about the Chao Zhou. It would have been better to follow his example. Thanks to his cross eyes, he saw two sides to life. For life is always what we see. He is Chinese. He understands the Chinese better than I do. He knows Liem the Chinese, and he avoided him. It was the Chao Zhou who pushed me into the rat trap, but I will leave him to his sweet dreams filled with tables and chairs. Another path awaits me. Let them call me an ingrate. At the end of the day, after this parting of ways, who can say which of the two of us is luckier? At the end of the day, our sufferings were the hidden part of the iceberg, the immense illusion we had created to deceive our hunger.

And I often thought of Chu. For a long time I would remember, with bitterness, those rotten spareribs, the cigarette lighter that clicked open, the shuddering of her body. Never again in this life will I taste happiness. Never.

Translated by Phan Huy Duong and Nina McPherson

A STAGNANT WATER PLACE

The Giang

A rainy night at Vinh station. A straw hut nestled on the roadside, water behind, half pond, half ditch, plenty of weeds and mosquitoes. The flame of an oil lamp flickering in the wind before the window. A skinny old dog covered with mud and chilled with the cold lies motionless in the shade of the lamp under the window, not daring to go in, for fear of being kicked. The wind plays, swirling around the door before slipping through in earnest. The straw roof rustles and whines. The croak of a tree frog calling to his mate keeps time with the rain . . .

This side of the window: "Trim the wick a little more, it doesn't need much oil."

That side of the window: "That's enough for people to see from far away."

A moment of silence.

This side: "What time is it?"

That side: "The watch has been sold . . . maybe nine or ten."

This side: "How much did you get for it?"

That side: "Cheapskate client, imitation watch, I only got sixty, lost ninety on the deal."

This side: "How? Why?"

That side: "A bargain at a hundred and eight, less thirty for the bite, had to pay him ninety."

This side: "Son of a bitch . . . Anyway, trim the wick . . ."

That side: "No need, I told you."

This side: "But . . . I'm afraid the ghosts might come back . . ."

"Quiet! So you said they might be back for more."

The sound of footsteps approaching, splashing through the water. A man's head pokes into the window, dripping all over the dog.

"How much?"

This side: "Fifty."

"Too much. Even Saigon girls don't cost that much."

"Then how much?"

"Twenty."

"Go fuck yourself. Save the twenty for your morning soup."

"Fucking whore!"

Footsteps clattering away.

"How about thirty?"

A voice replies: "Okay, it's raining, this may be the start of more deals later."

" . . ."

"Money first."

"What's your hurry? You're not being romantic."

"So you got the money?"

"Will you take rice?"

"What kind? Trade or New?"

"Monthly ration kind I just got. Just back from the service, haven't looked at it yet."

"So it's Trade rice. How much?"

"Twenty."

"Too expensive, and it's not a fair trade anyway."

"Eighteen then. Measure it out with this milk can."

"Yes, that's more convenient. No need to weigh, bought rice weighs more. No stones and gravel mixed in, right?"

"Check it out under the lamp."

"This rice is only fifteen."

"Don't heap it up in the can like that, I'll lose two kilos."

A ragged boy about nine years old suddenly appears as if he's popped up from underground. He stands there sucking his thumb, watching them measure out the rice. The man is trying to tie up his bag when the kid snatches the pouch of rice from the woman's hand and darts out.

The woman calls out after him: "Make rice, not soup . . . Remember to save some for me too."

Another head pokes in through the window: "Is this an inn by any chance?"

That side: "You've found the right place."

"By the half hour or by the night?"

"Either way you want."

The client sighs and comes in. "Any water to wash my feet?"

"The jar's right there under the porch."

"It's too dark. Can't you turn the wick a little higher?"

"There you go . . . Such beautiful eyes, and you leave them in the dark. What a shame!"

This side: "Drop the mosquito net."

"The roof leaks, the net is all wet."

"At least turn out the light then."

"There are other people here, ask them if they want it out."

" . . . "

"Take off your pants, you'll be more comfortable."

"Hmm . . . hmm . . . hmm . . ."

"Ow! That hurts, the buckle . . . Take off your pants."

That side: an exchange of whispers and muffled giggles.

This side: the clatter of the wooden horse in the stable.

" . . . "

Silence . . . The rain rattling on the straw roof . . . Slow breathing in the hut . . . Everything subsides into sleep.

That side: "Tired?"

"Satisfied?"

"What should I call you?"

"Been in Saigon long?"

"Reeducation camp prisoner, aren't you?"

"How'd you know?"

"How'd you know to come here?"

"Just got out. The pedicab man at the station showed me the way."

"Haven't gotten laid in quite a while, have you?"

"Eight years. Since '75."

"Married? Any children?"

"All gone to America."

"Take me to Saigon."

"I don't even know what I'm going to do there. How can I take care of you . . . Anyway, let's go over to the station and have some soup. Later on, we'll see."

This side: "How much do you take in?"

"Hard to tell, it varies."

"Married? Any children?"

". . ."

"Where do you come from?"

"Do Luong."

"What made you come here?"

"Life in the countryside is hard."

"Maybe. But isn't an honest life with a husband and kids better than this?"

"You a party member?"

"How did you know?"

"How many times have you done this?"

"This is the first time. Just to know what it's like."

"Like it?"

". . ."

"Aren't you afraid your comrades will find out?"

"I'm afraid people will find out, afraid of what the party would think, yes."

"Are you a party secretary?"

"Not yet. Just an assistant."

"How did you know to come here?"

"The secretary . . . that is, an acquaintance told me."

". . ."

"How long have you been in the trade?"

"Six years."

"A real pro. Any diseases?"

"I just got out from a 'reform.' Not long enough to get the clap yet."

"Up to your old tricks, huh? You must try harder to fight your wicked passions and think of your future. Shit, what's that?"

"Don't worry, it's only the dog. He's getting cold and scratching at the door to be let in."

"Thirty's too much, a quarter of the monthly payoff."

". . ."

"What's that?"

"Baked corn."

". . ."

"Only half, I haven't eaten."

The belt buckle clicks shut. The man checks his wallet and makes for the door with a bag of rice under his arm.

An old woman shuffles out from the inner room, one hand rubbing her knee, one hand patting her back. She holds up a piece of burning paper, twirls it around several times to chase the bad luck away. Then mustering all her strength, she lifts the washbasin and flings the dirty water out into the alley. The hut sinks back into darkness.

Translated by Cuong Nguyen

NINE DOWN MAKES TEN

Pham Thi Hoai

$\mathcal{T}$he first man in my unhappy life was slender and gentle, with an honest face. His was an honesty easy to find at any time, especially in people who have lived continually and without interruption in a sheltered environment. From an ordinary and uneventful childhood, to a college life, really no more than an extension of high school, and on to years as a government-employed technician, he displayed diligence, trustworthiness, and benevolence. It seemed that his was a kind of innate goodness, God-given, and protected. It seemed that he had always been righteous and good, but in a modest way, throughout a life untouched by self-doubt. I often thought of his goodness as a small thimble of fire, incapable of contributing much heat to the world, but occasionally heartwarming, though only in a symbolic way. And everyone, especially me, would strain toward this warmth; this effort would eventually become a habit and, later on, a moral imperative. Actually, by his side I could perhaps have lived the most suitable kind of life for a woman, in an apartment somewhere with that small flame. I'd give birth to well-fathered children and sit nightly clutching a ball of colorful wool, knitting colorful clothes, oblivious to self-doubt. Moreover, I would never fear unfaithfulness from him, as he could barely conceptualize adultery. But then I was too young, and I saw him as a sort of precious chessman, fortunate to have been moved by some unseen hand toward the safe squares and away from the violent battles. It seemed he would remain like this until a natural death finally seized him—and of course he'd remain honest, even in death. At that time, I considered my own birth some kind of cruel prank. I underestimated the size of his thimble of fire and failed to realize that his conventional honesty was no less believable than any other thing in life. Lacking skepticism, how could he understand science, art, religion, and in short, how could he understand love, which I considered the most fundamental craving for such a person as myself? I grew dissatisfied because he was too respectable and secure within his own respectability.

The second man was frivolous and merry, an urban child who had yet to go through the period of spiritual crisis characteristic of civilized society. He was crazy about music, from Beethoven to the Beatles, and possessed a good singing voice, but couldn't bear to practice. He also loved soccer and had a decent kicking foot but no concentration for workouts. Generally speaking, he had no concentration for anything, not even love. It's difficult to trust such a man, since it's never clear where the vectors of his personality are going. He seemed on first impression someone tremendously frivolous, one who possessed rare and peculiar notions of life, often puzzling to those who met him. His face was so natural it provoked suspicion, and I believed that under that wonderful skin lay hidden an extraordinary nature. How else to explain the perfect harmony existing between him and his environment, a final symbol of his capacity to live so deeply and so freely? But after only three sentences had been uttered from his lovely smiling mouth, this first impression quickly evaporated. He was one of a countless number of fortunate young men who live an unexamined life, not because of some conscious principle, but simply owing to circumstance—frivolity as a habit, as a way of life. He was frivolous in all details, and only details concerned him. His frivolity manifested itself in the care he took in striking a relaxed pose, and in the attention he devoted to celebrations, to feasting and to appearing knowledgeable; this all in the context of a larger existence that was not at all frivolous, but serious and substantial. At a certain age, those as extroverted and unaffected as he sink into the cloudy chaos of life's problems. Nevertheless, he was a person who brought me many pleasant hours, almost my happiest ever. I learned several important things from him, namely the discovery that I have a body and that it has a voice, a voice initially timid, then passionate, sometimes daring and profane, and progressively harder to please. He was the first man to show me that I am a woman, and for a long while after, how long I'm not sure, I remained grateful to this ordinary man. Life would certainly be impoverished if it lacked such merry and superficial men. Furthermore, he loved good food, and that truly is a worthwhile quality.

Man number three was around for less than a week but made me the most miserable. He was extremely handsome, so handsome that expressions of envy clogged the throats of those who met him. I immediately forgot who I was and experienced my first near-death state. After that I remained struck by a sensation both dangerous and seductive. This feeling has stayed with me throughout the remainder of my life, flooding and overwhelming smaller emotions, causing them to shrink and shrivel up. Recovery would demand a very large dose of optimism and an ability to adjust to new extremes. I knew that he was an inarticulate dullard, useless except for the ability to please the eyes, overreliant on his unusually gorgeous appearance, and frightfully uninteresting. But in his presence I completely forgot and forgave everything, although he was genuinely uncouth, foul, and cruel. After one week, I abandoned my urge not to indulge my self-pity and cried like a child whose toy has been stolen before she gets a chance to play with it. He would continue to be so gorgeous and useless for his entire life, and I, throughout my life, would flee from the desire to give myself to him, tormented by the absurdity of God and of myself even more. That affair was perhaps my only experience with true platonic love, especially the time I timidly ran my fingers through tufts of hair so beautiful they seemed not to belong to him and then abruptly jerked away as if stung by an electric shock.

After that I had an old man, experienced and worldly. He was born into a family whose members had participated for many generations in great historical events. They were thoughtfully educated, upwardly mobile, skilled at rubbing shoulders wherever they went, and never ruffled by callous twists and turns of fate. His handsomeness had a majestic air, and his every gesture suggested a profound awareness of his own value. I lived with him the longest, more than two years, and I grew much during this period. He knew how to answer all of my questions, whether about politics, love, religion, or the psychological taboos of bygone eras. He knew the way to sit crosslegged, drinking and composing poetry with literary friends; he was dignified and serious with academic friends, simple and easygoing with old women and children in the neighborhood, and brutish and cocky with the scum of the street. Many women revered him as some sort of idol. Old people found him loving and affectionate: he never said anything to hurt them. I enjoyed his generosity until it gradually became like a solid gold chain clamped around my neck. "What right do you have to be so generous?" I protested. And his answer suggested, "Just carry on with your life, little girl. You are still so small." Perhaps his brand of perfection was like a perfectly baked earthenware vase, adorned with brightly colored and well-proportioned designs; but its basic components, earth and rocks, originally loose, dirty and unformed, would remain essentially unchanged forever. In describing him, it's important to emphasize that he seemed profoundly satisfied with himself. Due to his advanced age and precious experience, plus a certain humorlessness, he did not dare or perhaps was unable to reject any part of the status quo. He gave me many things, or he almost gave me many things: affection to a nearly affectionate extent, warmth to a degree almost heartwarming. The whole of his perfect existence symbolized the limitless limitations of mankind. Not only did he unconditionally accept these limitations, but he used them to justify his behavior. He adroitly maintained a cozy family life while simultaneously offering his generosity to me. He explained that people are truly small creatures, fettered by their environment at birth and by various obligations as an adult. Thus they can maneuver only in a limited way and within the confines of some predetermined grid. I hated those grids and harshly mocked the way he struggled with his limitations. Up until the final moments, he still offered me a generous smile, and it seemed that compared with other men, he cared about me the most. Countless times thereafter, I longed to abandon my high-pressure work and relationships and run back to him, hiding my face in his solid chest and conceding that he has always been right. But I clicked my tongue and decided against it. This flexible man was considered exemplary by the successful members of society, but who really cares what they think?

Man number five was an idealist. He belonged to that breed of man not born for women, money, or pleasure, and this made me curious. My curiosity, however, did not last long, for contrary to my expectations, he was insipid and shallow. His ideal world—to be brought about by struggle either to reform educational science, protect the environment, or reestablish a tradition of sarong-wearing among the ethnic minorities (what a big deal!)—perhaps could really exist someday. I never doubted its attractiveness, and sometimes, in a highly inspired state, he could transmit a bit of his passion and emotion to nonbelievers. But in general his view of life suggested a narrow corridor that was periodically repainted but remained cramped and dreary. In a calculating way, I studied and applied tactics of love, and bearing the costs of lost time and more annoyance than happiness, I contrived to probe the bulwarks of his idealism, to test its endurance. This plunged him into an overwhelming spiritual crisis. Friends took him to an emergency room, where his deeply self-tortured soul was inflicted with tens of thousands of units of antibiotics, and just because he could not choose between his love and his ideals. He was the kind of person who possesses only enough internal strength to devote himself to one thing at a time. Leaving the hospital, he embarrassingly thanked me and disappeared down one of his mysterious corridors, this one concerned with the public reform of morning exercises for people too physically unfit to work. However, my calibrated burst of love had misfired, and his ideals gave him an easy way out. That was the only affair in which I actively played the role of the seductress from beginning to end, and after he was gone I was genuinely sad and regretful. After thinking a while, it became clear that he had chosen his dreary and narrow world over me. A lesson for simple curiosity. But I must admit he was the purest man I have ever met.

The sixth man was extremely complex, almost irrationally so, in the context of this most poor and backward society. When I met him, he had achieved an undeniable level of prestige in the diminutive intellectual world of Hanoi, a place where one can meet the most famous people without a prior appointment and use intimate terms of address within the first moments of striking up a conversation. I immediately surrendered before him—this human labyrinth, this infinitely dimensional zone cluttered with the disorder of contradictions, ideology, experience and ambition. But I couldn't help wondering: Do all these interesting and complicated things really exist, or are they only an expensive and ultimately meaningless drama that people feel compelled to stage in order to cope with their fellow men and themselves? Conventional geniuses never seem to have personalities; who would dare say that Shakespeare, for example, was melancholy, bitter, or sharp-tongued? Therefore I concluded that my sixth man was no genius. He had too much personality and was too worried about his originality. His complexity seemed the natural outgrowth of the uncontrolled interaction between two currents. On the one hand was the traditional educational system, in which the value of everything— romanticism, historical method, even the slipping of cushions under the bed before a night of lovemaking—is fixed according to a guaranteed standard of truth, goodness and beauty. And on the other hand was real life: vivid, crowded, subverting all conventions regarding of tradition, undermining all ideologies, and naturally overturning all values. Because he was sensitive, he found it hard to overlook clashes between the two, but because he was at the same time intelligent, he refused to take sides. Gradually he found that the best way out was to situate himself somewhere above the fray and contentedly gaze down. Consequently, people who participated in increasingly public discussions claimed that in fact he systematically rejected everything. They were wrong. He was too complicated and lost in his own complexity to reject everything. However, he did become a somewhat legendary and original figure, and as people stood anxious and sweaty in his presence, time passed and I grew tired. During the time I lived with him, I tended to dwell obsessively on my own sadness. I uttered strange and often contradictory phrases, ate and dressed on purpose in a slovenly manner, and lavished praise on only those books that no one understood. When we broke up, I felt the world to be shallow and its people superficial. It seemed that I never received from this famous man a soulful kiss, meaning one both natural and pure. Afterward, I heard that he had become a radical moralist, preaching about the nature of three distinct roads: the acceptance of, rejection of, and escape from conventional morality. Later on he became a kind of popular sage, a dialectician who approached society's intricate problems through dialectical methods and by applying extracts of oriental and occidental knowledge. In the end he became a recluse, and in an unrelated development, the intellectual life of Hanoi contracted, and no one spoke further of him.

The seventh man brought me much excitement but also my moments of greatest uneasiness. He was not unusually attractive: short, with thinning hair and a small forehead. Only his voice was exquisite, deep, melodious, and full of unforeseen contingencies. Upon hearing his voice, difficult-to-please listeners, even those impressed only by outward appearance, would be riveted and believe that before them was, if not a genius in disguise, some sort of otherworldly species of man, a being who used this earth only as a temporary dwelling. Or perhaps they would feel that this small man must deeply understand the quintessence of life, as if his existence had spanned scores of generations and consequently could draw on the experience of both ghosts and men. It was said that he followed nihilistic principles, but I didn't understand what this meant. I speculated that it was a unique philosophical idea that could never be fully grasped, or perhaps the final foundation of all foundations, or a mode of behavior reserved especially for those without virtue, those both unhappy and very lonely. But this man refused to advertise his noble misery, the pain he felt for humanity, the loneliness in his blood or the weariness with which he experienced the age. On the contrary, his expression suggested contentment and freedom from worry, the capacity to accept or reject circumstances with equal ease; and sometimes he was simply difficult to read. His one fascination was with the brevity of human existence, and the only being who provoked him to fits of anger and an enduring sensation of confusion and helplessness was God. He considered God to be his only worthwhile rival and lamented the fact that the great one so rarely showed himself. It was perhaps the complexity of his relationship with God that fundamentally distinguished him from the mass of nihilists in the movement. Their lazy activism was habitually insignificant, and they always seemed prepared to shout "I've found it!" after taking only a half step out the door.

It was not easy to label him godless, immoral, or relativistic, and finally one could say that he had a great sense of humor, his genius lying with his comic gifts. Many women went out with him. This small Don Juan was thoughtful and considerate toward them, and because of his skill in the various stages of love affairs, he earned a sultry reputation. After studying with him, many miserable women left, and turning on him, denounced what they had learned. I also left him, after admitting to myself that I was to remain a weak woman and would spend my entire life searching for strength outside of myself. In my present state of panic I dare not enter into his zone, a zone wonderful for creating poetry and philosophy but inappropriate for comforting the hearts of women. I'm afraid that I will forever grieve over this unhappy Don Juan, and I can drive away my sadness only by shrugging my shoulders and saying, "He was really pitiable: no emotion, no passion, no faith; in short, he didn't know what to live for."

The eighth man had the hair of a poet, the face of a poet, and a soul especially given over to poetry. Such qualities are found only in people who have a lot of time and no concrete obligations toward life. When engrossed in the rising and falling of his watery waves, and once acquainted with his passionate love of writing—swiftly, without semicolons—I began to understand that the most worthwhile obsession is an obsession that is actually independent of the object of fixation. The object is only borrowed as a pretext, a means, an environment, through which or in which the obsessed person can project his own eternal and essential hunger, thus fulfilling the requirements of death—the dissolution of the ego for something, anything, that exists independently outside of one's self. Perhaps that obsession should be controlled. At some point the most mundane catalyst, a skirt or a fallen leaf, is enough to provoke a series of captivating chain reactions, while at another time much more important objects will inspire only an absurd indifference. I did not know whether I was worthwhile or mundane, but this was not really the issue. I was grateful to this man and enjoyed the taste of his affection, despite a small stubborn girl within me who refused to cooperate. She said: According to this particular mode of obsession all objects are equal, and therefore I am no different from a potato or an ant, but if people like to manufacture an obsession by constantly stoking their own engine, then by all means they should go ahead. Gradually I learned to repress that obstinate girl and ignore my uneasiness with the difference between artificially produced obsessions and primeval obsessions. Let Proust distinguish between the two, or the column "Mothers Advise Daughters" in some women's magazine; I am interested only in my own obsession and its consequences. The most ironic aspect of its unforeseen consequences was that both he and I became pitiful victims of the obsession. It forced him to wait by every street on which I might pass, to pull me away from all activities, no matter how fundamental to existence: eating, sleeping, seeking work; it interfered with all my relationships, with my family, colleagues, friends, and expanded into all areas and times that I liked to save to myself. I no longer had my own space, time or lifestyle; my environment was upset, my psychological state was upset, my language went out of my control. The obsession was like a third character in a love triangle leading him and poking me in the back; it followed its own dizzying trajectory and changed obstinate people into slaves, oblivious to their limited abilities. In short, it swallowed us without chewing: he failed his examinations, unable to resist the rush toward inertia, and I turned blind, like a Chinese lantern at a festival. In this situation, people can't help but grate on and annoy each other. The demands of individual liberation eventually transform society into a mass of "I"s, each one desiring to control the others. This naturally provokes conflict. Exhausted after such a time-consuming conflict, he abandoned the relationship for the call of religion, but this new obsession exacted an even higher price. I returned to my original form of a potato or maybe an ant, and heaved a sigh of relief. I felt sorry for God or Buddha, as this poet would certainly grate on them. But perhaps those two gentlemen understand the essence of life better than I and can look beyond him.

The ninth man was a man of action, few words, forthrightness, and pragmatism. He was intelligent, decently educated, and sensitive enough to appreciate the real value of such nonmaterial activities as wordplay, pipe dreams, fortunetelling, or making love. However, the road he chose for himself satisfied a predilection for certitude and controlled vigilance. He believed in no one, entrusted himself to no one, and struggled to force life itself to bend to his will. His profound desire to conquer life was impressive, vaguely like Don Quixote's, both desperate and dauntless. He had held down many jobs, for many different reasons, ranging from the desire to secure life's basic necessities to attempts to secure glory and power. But he was rarely satisfied, as work never quite met his expectations. The only measure he took seriously was that of practical advantage, immediate material gain being optimal and the forging of useful future connections merely acceptable. He was strict and prompt in the repayment of debts. While people found him useful, they were often cool toward him because he was completely lacking in false ethics, those gastric juices that allow for the digestion of the inedible components in the relations between people. He promised little, yet was so helpful with my unhappy life's most pressing problems (more so than all the other men combined), that during those moments of satisfaction and gratitude I confusedly asked myself if this really could be love. And could women like myself have lost such confidence in themselves and in this difficult-to-understand era that we need such a love as this? He did grant me three things: First, because he was always so busy, he did not have the time to undergo a period of spiritual crisis, something that I had already been blessed with enough times before; as relations with women never took up his whole life, I enjoyed a notable degree of freedom; and third, with him I suddenly felt a daily sensation of being deeply and snugly attached to my life, a sensation that I had thought about many times before but never actually experienced. I grew stronger and more contented, and began to seriously consider the prospect of marrying him. Life with such a thoroughly practical man would certainly promise a measure of success, like entering into a contract in which each side does not sap the other's vitality, as often happens with those claiming to be madly in love. There is certainly some advantage in avoiding excessive closeness and coolly carrying out contractual provisions. At our final meeting, he said, "In all areas including marriage, I am always faithful to a single measure of value: practical advantage." And on considering this measure, he determined that I was not the one to satisfy his requirements. Now he must bear the responsibility for his heartlessness.

Enough. He was the ninth man.

Translated by Peter Zinoman

MEN, WOMEN AND FLOWERS

Duc Ban

$\mathcal{T}$wo men were riding on a sun-splashed street on a summer afternoon. No one knows their names, ages, or where they're from. Even the writer of this story doesn't; let's just call them "a man wearing a hat" and "a bareheaded man."

Both of them steered onto the sidewalk and stepped into a small café under the almond tree. Inside the café it was dim, cool, and smelled vaguely of peppermint. The proprietress was a delicate woman wearing a thin yellow silk blouse, her hair as soft as water. Her eyes were extremely black; even the most hard-to-please person on earth would not find fault with them. Beautiful and soaked in a pure sadness.

"Hello, Sister," the two men said, the voices latching onto each other and trembling slightly.

The woman arched her brows and nodded, a magnanimous and somewhat noble gesture.

The two young men sat at the table by the door.

The bareheaded man stretched an arm across the back of his chair.

The man wearing a hat folded his arm across his chest.

A swarm of flies buzzed around them, then landed in a

heart-shaped puddle on the table. Their many legs dipping into a liquid the color of wood. Then they stretched their wings and swooped up, sprinkling the air, and the men's pants, with tiny dots of liquid the size of pinpricks.

"There's a smell of honey," the man wearing a hat said, sniffing.

"Some sort of incense," the bareheaded man said pensively.

A moment of deep silence.

The young man wearing a hat shook his sleeve, writhed, then yelled: "Flies! Flies!"

The woman laughed.

The bareheaded man draped his entire body onto the table. He thought of the laugh of a woman from a fairy tale, a laugh he heard in his imagination when he was seventeen . . . An errant knight chased after that laugh from the time he was a young man until his hair was gray. He died one evening as the sun was setting into the ocean. In waves, the woman's laughter lapped over him like a funereal shroud.

The man wearing a hat shuddered suddenly. Lines appeared on his face. Two flies were casually crawling on his ringed fingers. He stood up, stomped on the floor, then stepped outside the café.

"Can't stand this!" he fumed. Whether he was furious at the flies or something else no one knows.

"Just like in the fairy tale," the bareheaded man was still pensive. He appeared exactly like a sleepwalker. His eyes were wet. Tears flowed in rivulets down his slowly reddening cheeks. They were such strange kinds of tears that the flies flew off.

The woman looked into the distance. Her succulent lips, as red as lotus flowers, stammered suddenly as she asked the young man, who was now standing right in front of her, separated by a mere hand span:

"Do you like Raphael's painting, 'Poseidon and Circe'?"

The bareheaded man tilted his head to look through the hole in the thatch roof. He was readying himself for a flight into the sunlight and clouds.

It is told, they later became husband and wife.

As for the young man wearing a hat, he became a breeder of a special kind of birds that feeds only on flies.

Translated by Linh Dinh

IN THE
RECOVERY ROOM

Mai Kim Ngoc

1.

"*T*hanks for coming to see me. Thanks for everything. There's no one to talk to in this hospital; it gets lonely . . .

"You lived in Hue for a long time, no? Back when you came to visit Dung, you were in ninth grade, weren't you? Time flies. Now even your kids are married. Me, I'm old, so old . . .

"What time will they operate on me tomorrow, do you know? . . . Is it eight? Maybe the nurse will wake me up before then . . .

"That nurse Kelly came to prepare me for the operation a while ago. She was shaving me, and she said the hair on my chest was denser than on a true American . . . She used up two Bic shavers to do the job . . . You don't know how many women have fallen for this chest of hair, what a shame . . .

"With you, I can talk about anything. Our relationship is kind of strange, don't you think? I know you're different from me in many ways, but you still respect me. The other thing is, since you married Trang, you should be addressing me as father . . .

"But I think you and I, we can't be calling each other dad and son, not only because we're used to calling each other uncle and nephew before, when you were still finishing high school. But I feel that it would ruin our relationship if we were to call each other dad and son.

"Between uncle and nephew, we can talk about everything, including stuff about men and women. Fathers and sons have their problems, it's not like they can be totally open with each other. Trang's the same way. She's always treating me as though, outside of my duties as a father, I have no other life. She's always resented me. She doesn't say more than a thousand words to me in a year, shorter than a page of your short stories.

"Sit, do sit down . . .

"I'm not afraid of dying. I'm going to live longer than those they say have the longevity of Co Lai Hy. You know, when you took me to Dr. Hung, I had not wanted to have an operation. But all of you told me to go ahead with the operation. My friends at the Elderly Association too . . . They're like you, they keep saying I may be old but I still have a strong body, with the heart of someone in his fifties, the cancer growth is still new, get rid of it and I'd be all right. After the operation, I'd still have enough of my lungs left to live on, easily. Of course, I'd have to give up tennis, but I'll still be able to do all other things . . .

"Are you laughing at me? I know what you're thinking. Are you laughing because I said 'other things'? You're like Trang, always accusing me of being a playboy. Heaven gives me strength; Heaven gives me more life force than other people; even if I didn't want to, I'd still have to be a playboy . . .

"But I'm only a playboy because I love my wife, you know. Look at her, all these years, she's never been anything but skin and bones . . . That's why after she gave birth to Trang, I had to abstain. Back then there was no medicine, abstaining meant going with the moon; in a whole month, only the four days before and the four days afterward would be safe . . . The stuff between wife and husband, I volunteered to cut back to a fourth of what's normal. But if you love your wife, that's what you have to do . . .

"*Qui veut aller loin menage sa monture,* the French used to say. You've been in America for too long, you probably don't remember your French. It just means on a long road, you must let your horse rest. Husband and wife, we have a hundred years together. You can't just be hopping on, galloping always, no horse can stand it . . .

"Oh, I forget, your French is still very good . . . I remember when I dropped that wonderful aphorism in front of my wife, you understood it and told me to be careful or she would be sad . . .

"Trang thinks you're sensitive . . . But I think that it's not always a good thing to be sensitive. I'll be frank, your sensitivity can make life so dull.

"That story about the horse on a long road, your aunt didn't mind, she even liked it. Don't you remember, at the dinner table that day, there were people who didn't understand, I had to point directly at my wife to introduce her clearly: *Voici ma monture.* She didn't protest, she even smiled.

"You think she laughed out of embarrassment, or to hide her sadness? Your kids are married but you still don't understand women. Women like to be squashed, they like to be mounted, don't you know? They told me so . . .

"You're blushing again . . .

"You look just like your wife when you scrunch up your nose like that. I know you two think of me as a dirty old man . . .

"So you want to talk about something else, huh?

"OK then. We can talk about literature. Oh, I read your story about Hue carefully. Can I be frank?

"You write from the outside, as though someone not from Hue was writing about Hue. How can you write about the River of Perfume without writing about the sampans of Hue?

"Please, don't argue with this poor man. I'm old but not senile . . . Sure, you wrote about the sampans, but you were still too chaste about it. You didn't get at the heart of what the sampans meant. You didn't write about spending the night on a sampan. That's bad . . .

"The story about the sampan on the Perfume River is like a *riec* fish from the pond, you get one out, it would still be thrashing about, its mouth still gasping for air, its scales lustrous like silver, its fins flapping like the wings of a sparrow . . . Instead of serving it raw for me to eat in a salad, you prepared it as a stuffed dead fish with glazed eyes and a stiff body; worse yet, it no longer smells like a fish. It's like a fish to put in an aquarium for display in the living room . . .

"You've never experienced it? You've never set foot on a sampan? So you were still a virgin then. Poor Trang. That means my little daughter's wedding night didn't amount to much . . . What can you do if both bride and groom are so clueless?

"Back to literature . . .

"Since you have no life experience, I'll give you some. Let me tell you about the first time I went on a sampan. Only the first time now . . . Ha, ha, what those damn poets often refer to as the first steps.

"You have to imagine Hue of the old days, before you were born, Hue in my time, Hue from the times of *Les Amis du Vieux Hue*. I was a philosophy major at Khai Dinh then, just engaged to your aunt . . .

"She was a princess, a mandarin's daughter, a beauty queen of the capital, sheltered behind closed doors and high walls, from a very strict family. But after the engagement, Trang's maternal family relaxed. We were always chaperoned when we went to the movies. But whenever I came by their house, they basically left us alone . . .

"When there were adult visitors, Trang's grandmother, pretending she needed the living room for the elders, allowed her daughter to receive her husband-to-be in her room upstairs. Sure we kept the door ajar, but we were pretty free, because the staircase had several wooden steps that squeaked, and no one in the family would just barge into anyone else's room . . .

"But our liberty had its limits . . . After such visits, I would go home in so much pain. It would be better had there been no freedom at all, a halfway kind of freedom is just painful.

These things, it's better to go without completely. That's kinder than allowing people to taste just a little, you can smell it, but you're left wanting . . .

"You're blushing again . . . You and Trang are such a perfect couple, always scrunching your faces up whenever I speak of pleasures . . . But you two aren't all that innocent, how many kids do you have, six or seven . . . and what about you guys popping out three kids in two years? Such hypocrites.

"I'm only kidding, don't hold a grudge against me. Let me start my story . . .

"Once after I visited my fiancée, I was neither satisfied nor hungry. I decided to go on a sampan. You have to know, in my situation back then, that was no easy decision . . .

"I had some precocious friends, and I knew from them that the sampans on the Perfume River were floating hotel rooms, and in each of those rooms there would be a woman ready to sell what a man wanted to buy. When I heard my friends' stories, I imagined the cabins in the sampans to be secretive places that held all the mystery and seduction of the forbidden fruits from ancient days . . .

"I had several dreams about the things that were inside such sampans, scenes of comfortable bedding, soft music, women as beautiful as mythical ghosts, I couldn't remember their faces when I woke up, all I remembered were the bodies and limbs as delicate as a pine branch with starkly white bark, and I remembered that uneasy feeling of being both ashamed and proud of being a man.

"Sometimes, I would dream about your aunt on the sampan, and completing the path to ecstasy with her which I had to abandon during the day . . . At such times, I'd wake up and feel real guilty toward my fiancée. And to make up for it, I tried to keep my virginity for my wife . . .

"But that night, after I left Trang's grandfather's house, I was determined to go on a sampan. Maybe because there was a full moon. You work in the sciences, maybe you understand the reason . . .

"It's true, you know, when there was a full moon, I just couldn't sleep, even now, at my age, it's still like that sometimes. Even if I am lying down inside, without being able to see the moon, I feel something outside is calling me . . . It's as if I'm in tune with the moon's occult influences and have to struggle with suppressed passions that no longer have any shape or form . . . But that's being too poetic. Don't think I am getting metaphysical or mystical on you. Actually, the darkest impulse is when you want sex but you can't have it.

"You say the moon has its own pull? You're probably right. 'Cause I'd read somewhere that originally man was a fish. Perhaps in a full moon, the blood in the heart and the veins suddenly is reminded of its ancient roots, which is the sea, and just like the sea, it boils over with sexual desire, like a tidal wave . . . Huh. Maybe heaven gave me blood that's more sensitive to the moon than all these feeble men . . .

"But let me continue the story of sleeping on the sampan . . .

"I was going past the docks at Thua Phu, the pine trees at the end of the garden caught my eyes. Like I told you, every time I saw a pine tree with the white bark under the moonlight, I thought of naked women . . .

"But this time I wasn't thinking of just women in general, I was thinking about your aunt, not totally naked, only half-naked, like what was tacitly permissible during those days between two people who have been promised to each other.

"I went straight to the sampans moored under the branches of the ancient tree. I called out to the sampan anchored at the outer edge. The second time I called out, I heard sheets and blankets being moved, then at last a woman's sleepy voice invited me aboard . . .

"I must confess that the moment I stepped into the cabin, my dreams were shattered. I only saw how poor and tattered everything was. The flower of sin didn't seem as magical as I had expected, and the scene inside the sampan seemed disorderly and old, like the dirty intestines of a capital city. From the damp smell of the blankets to the wrinkled clothes of the woman, everything was repulsive to me.

"I wanted to go back on shore, regretting that I had rented the sampan for the entire night rather than by the hour. But the woman had rowed the boat out to the middle of the river.

"She rowed upstream toward the White Tiger Bridge. When she had reached some distance, she anchored the boat and crawled into the cabin with me.

"As if she was trying to create some kind of atmosphere, she sang for me. She sang the song 'A Thousand Miles of Our Nation.' She didn't have a voice, the singing was aimless and overwrought, desperate for the support of a lute or a clapping block. Her tiredness seemed to mock the noble content of the song, and it was outrageously funny that she should compare herself to Princess Tran Huyen Tran, Empress of Champa . . .

"I sat quietly to listen to her sing, not finding it any good, but I was thinking of her pitiful attempt at being fair, to give me my money's worth . . . I was reminded of the woman who was my neighbor at my apartment, a housewife who liked to sing poetry, but without any talent whatsoever. I hung on to the out-of-sync singing of the woman on the Perfume River as something banal, thus normal, in order to domesticate the vulgar environment . . .

"The repulsion subsided, I felt the pressure lessening, and I began to feel pity. I relaxed and the woman too relaxed. When I admitted it was my first time on a sampan, she became very happy, thinking my impassivity was due to shyness. With more confidence, she helped me enthusiastically like a kindergarten teacher breaking in a new student. Thanks to her attentiveness and professionalism, the merchandise was consumed at last.

"A while later, lying next to her, I looked out at the river. The moon had moved up high, but it was faint as a red ball in the mist. It was quiet around, and I was surprised to feel a sense of comfort spreading throughout my body. I thought things between a man and a woman, if they happened in a romantic situation, or gracefully, or with total understanding, would be so satisfying, wonderful . . . But when it's so naked, so unromantic, without love, without mutual understanding as it was between me and the prostitute, it was, in fact, not all that bad. More or less, you can say it was pleasing. I must state that straight out . . .

"She leaned on her elbow, tilted her head to look at me. She said, 'What are you thinking, Brother? Men who have just lost their virginity are so funny. Look at you lying there so dazed, you're so lovely . . . I'm telling you the truth . . .' Then suddenly, she leaned over, kissed me on the mouth. The stench of her breath spread over my face, and under the egg-shaped lamp in the corner of the boat, I could see her yellowed and dirty row of teeth. Now I was feeling filthy.

"I was able earlier to repress the repulsion I was feeling, but now it came up again. I felt overwhelmed by the stench of human sweat, of filth, of semen from all the men who had been on the sampan, who had used the sheets and mats, who had used the woman's body before. From the damp fabric of the pillow, I could smell the stench of dried saliva that had collected there for who knows how long. My stomach was boiling like a man who had swallowed poison. I thought of the woman's kiss, and her slippery tongue that felt like an uncooked fish, and the bile came up from my throat and filled up my mouth. I got up and rushed to the side of the sampan and threw up all over.

"My stomach was all knotted up as though it wanted to wring all of its contents out. In the cold night, I heard the sound of my vomit plopping into the water, the vulgar sound of man's pitiful essence. My blood was pulsating in my temples, but beating quite slowly, and getting slower and slower, as though about to stop. My limbs were listless; I collapsed on my back. I was freezing. It was a cold coming from the pit of my stomach, like bits of ice cubes were traveling through my veins.

"It was as if I had left my body and could see myself lying

dead on the wood surface at the bottom of the sampan, and the mist had covered most of the surface of the river, and there were just a few lights still flickering among the fishing boats on the far side . . . I thought I was about to die, and death seemed comfortable and there was nothing to be scared of . . .

"Somewhere in the fog, a heron let out a lonely cry . . . The cry roused me, and I thought I was dying a silent, shameful death. I sat up; my youth was violently and desperately protesting against the coldness and death that was invading both my spirit and my body . . .

"Suddenly someone stuck a pin into the flesh around my tailbone, the sharp pain woke me up. A pair of hands started to massage my chest . . . I could smell eucalyptus balm, and the pair of hands went on to massage my back, my belly, my arms and legs. There was warmth wherever the hands went, and I felt soothed as life reentered my body through the warmth. Half awake, half dead, I imagined your aunt's aristocratic face fussing over me, and I closed my eyes, believing I would be revived. Although I had a splitting headache, I was happy for it, as if the pain was chasing death and the coldness away . . .

"I finally came to. Under my back I felt the sand that had collected on the mat, from the shoes of all those men who had been there before, I suppose. I knew I was in the cabin, she must have dragged me in there.

"I could smell again the odor of the sheets. The stench coming from the pillow invaded my nostrils, but instead of being revolted, I inhaled it, instinctively. I felt a sweetness in my lungs. The stench was no longer a stench, but an emblem of life, its vitality. I welcomed it with the joy of someone returning from the frigid land of the dead.

"I opened my eyes. The prostitute was using a colonial coin to rub more eucalyptus balm into my back. You know that coin? It's about the size of a dollar coin, but it was red copper. It must have been hard for her, her shirt was soaking wet and stuck to her flat chest, and her forehead glistened with sweat. I reached up to undo the buttons of her shirt. I looked at her pair of breasts, they were beginning to wilt like lotus at the end of summer, and I thought they were beautiful. Without seeming to pay attention to me directly, she said, 'My little brother's awake.'

"I asked her about the scar on the right breast, at about the nine o'clock position, real round, a star with eight points . . . She went on to rub the eucalyptus balm on me, and said, 'The Legionnaire burnt Elder Sister with a cigarette . . .' Her voice stayed calm, as though she was talking about an insignificant cut on her finger that had happened long before while she was preparing food, and she seemed to be concentrating only on my well-being.

"Under the light of the egg-shaped lamp she had just turned up, the prostitute seemed different somehow, not only because she had changed the way she was addressing me, referring to herself now as my older sister rather than a younger one . . . She smiled, her teeth were dry and her lips were taut, like those of a harvest girl under the midday sun in July . . . The lips and teeth weren't so repulsive anymore, like they had been just a few hours earlier, but they now reminded me of a pleasant time when I was inspecting the rice stalks in my grandfather's fields in a summer afternoon.

"All of a sudden, she changed. It wasn't the light from the egg-shaped lamp any more, but it was some inner light that glowed on her face, showing off a beauty that had been hidden before, in her hair, her ears, her eyes, her nose, on the skin of her cheeks, on her eyebrows . . . She looked exactly like, not my fiancée, but the cousin who took care of me whenever I visited my mother's family in the country. She and I had been close since we were kids, and we stayed close even when we got older, to the point of worrying our mothers . . .

"Why are you staring at me like that? Don't get any wrong ideas. I am not one to commit incest. Even in the middle of nature, even though we both weren't unfamiliar with scenes of pigs, roosters, and chickens coupling all over the place on my grandmother's farm. During full-moon nights when I went with her to bathe in the spring, I never had any bad thoughts . . . Looking at her in her wet clothes under the moon, I only thought how beautiful she was and decided that when I was older, I would marry someone just as beautiful.

"Back to the prostitute . . .

"She said, 'Listen to me, little brother, stop going to whores.' The word 'whores' made me uncomfortable, but I was too tired to argue, so I closed my eyes and went back to sleep. When she pulled the cover up to my chin, I smelled again the human odor that had accumulated there and felt the heat of the eucalyptus balm on my back, chest, and lower belly, and it was very soothing. You could call it a kind of happiness . . .

"Near morning, I opened my eyes and she was still sitting there, watching over me. She went to the gas stove at the end of the sampan to heat up the chicken soup she must have brought the night before. I thought her custom was to offer her guests a bowl of chicken soup . . . When I finished the one bowl, she poured out the rest of the soup for me. 'Eat, little brother, get your strength back. I'm not hungry,' she told me. After I finished, I was sweating, and she dried me with a cloth, then rubbed more balm on me . . .

"When I woke up again, the sampan had docked, and the woman had left. I got dressed and crawled out of the cabin, realizing I was at the Dong Ba instead of the Thua Phu docks. I was sorry I couldn't say goodbye to her.

"I walked along the river toward the market and thought the morning was very refreshing, and life beautiful. I felt much more at ease than before I had gone on that sampan. What's stranger still, I felt even more at ease than when I had left my fiancée's home.

"I thought, because of the woman on the Perfume River, I had learned so many new things, from the bestial but calming pleasure after you've made love, to the devastating coldness of someone who had just died, to the unexpected sweetness of sweat odor once I had been revived. I couldn't believe a person's face, even a prostitute's face, could be so tender and noble, like an angel's . . .

"Funny how I thought the prostitute resembled the French woman who taught me French. It wasn't that her face looked like the face of my teacher, because my teacher was not only sophisticated but also very young, very attractive. She resembled her just because the French woman used to teach me about life's beauty through her language lectures . . .

"The thing was, she was bound by theories of syntax and grammar. Maybe her language was too formal, too academic, so when she talked to her students about the preciousness of life, real life had already wilted and died in her lectures. There was no way she could have taught me that when you come back from the dead, the most miserable life could be as beautiful as a dream, and the human odor in the sheets and covers could be as sweet as the best fresh orange juice . . .

"You think I'm being flowery? Surely, I'm not always vulgar, and I am capable of good thoughts about women. I can praise women with words just as pure as the ones in your corny novels . . .

"That's not true?

"So you resent me . . . You don't want to write my story . . . You're being circuitous, but I still understand you think that my viewpoint is an affront to the dignity of women . . .

"You think I'm wrong, considering a prostitute as a lady and a proper lady like a prostitute . . . But who's a proper lady? Are you talking about your aunt or the French teacher?

"Your tongue's sharp, like Trang's. Funny how only you two dare to be so disrespectful of me . . . No matter, it's what I was thinking at the time . . .

"When I was walking past the Dong Ba market, the smell coming from Café Phan made me hungry. The two bowls of chicken soup the woman gave me had been digested. I went inside, ordered a coffee and a sandwich, but when I reached inside my pocket, my wallet was gone. I rushed back to the dock, but the sampan wasn't there anymore. I remembered that during the night, when I was nearly awake, I had seen her messing with my clothes, which I had thrown all over the cabin.

"I thought of the word 'whore,' which she had used to call herself, and I considered reporting her to the police. But I changed my mind. Still being romantic, I thought she was the embodiment of life. I promised myself not to report her. Who would be stupid enough to hand life over to the police?

"In the end, I had to go to the police, because of all the papers and money I had in my wallet. A week later, a policeman came to my house and asked me to go to the station to identify the culprit. I wasn't home, so the police left a warrant for me. I thought I'd go to the station to reclaim my wallet, give her some money and ask the police to let her go.

"But the following day, the Japanese staged a coup against the French, and I couldn't make it to the police station until a week later. The French police chief had been thrown in jail with a bunch of assistants. The police were being reorganized under the Tran Trong Kim regime, and everyone was busy with a new order, a new national anthem, a new flag, no one remembered whether the thieving prostitute had been released or whether she had been handed over to the Japanese police, to be sent to a whorehouse for Japanese soldiers. The books had been burned, and no one knew how to find her . . .

"You need to go to work now? Go on. Come back this afternoon if you're free . . ."

2.

"Tung, about my operation . . . Do you think there's any danger? I'll live, right? Tell me the truth . . . You already know I am not afraid of dying. I wasn't even afraid when I almost died on the sampan that night. I was just cold, it was the coldness of the dead . . .

"And now, it's cold even among the living . . . Look at these sheets. The Americans clean them so well, they're so white. I can only smell detergent on them.

"Tung, give me a glass of wine.

"It's on the table . . . I had to beg for it . . . The doctor had to order the nurses, reasoning that a bit of wine tonight would actually be helpful. Do you like wine? I love it, back when I was sent to France for work. There's nothing as wonderful as a good bottle of wine and a tray with all kinds of cheese . . .

"By the way, Tung, these sheets and blankets . . . how many people do you think have used them? Some are dead, some still alive. Some had internal wounds, some external . . . even women needing gynecological care . . .

"But there isn't a drop of blood from the guy in a car accident, not a stain from a mother just before she gives birth, not even a urine stain from an old man, half-paralyzed. Everything is so white and smells so good . . .

"I understand what you're saying . . . Sure, they have to sterilize it, to make sure there's no contamination. But it's so sterilized, washed so clean, there's nothing left of the lives that have passed through here, the people who have used these blankets and sheets before me . . .

"I feel that I am going to die.

"Don't worry about me saying such a thing. Between us, uncle and nephew, there is nothing we can't talk about . . . I am not saying evil things . . .

"There are a lot of premonitions . . .

"First, in the past year, I have seen almost all the women who have slept with me . . . Maybe a hundred . . . Each in a different job, a different situation, and each of them has disappointed me when we saw each other again . . . No one is doing badly. You can even say some are pretty successful . . .

"But when I see my old lovers' faces, I notice that what had mesmerized me in the past, whether it's in the corner of their eyes, or their smile or their mannerism . . . had all been washed out by what they've gone through after we split up, washed out to the point where I can't even recognize them . . . In their old age they have lost whatever that was distinctive about them, so that they all look the same, as if they're sisters . . .

"Actually, it's not that I'm disappointed with them, it's more with life . . . You don't understand? It's like this, each of these women, until we met again, represented a path my life could have taken. Each of them, had I lived with them longer, would have led me toward different pleasures, different discoveries about life . . . A traveler can't turn at every crossroads, but once he's home, he still has the pleasure of knowing the world promises other things he has not seen, which he can see later . . . But when you find out every road leads to Rome, you're bound to be disappointed.

"The trouble with me when I meet these old lovers again is just that . . . An old woman is just an old woman . . . At the end of your life, it doesn't matter which old woman you end up with . . . How many people can still find the earlier distinctiveness in their old woman?

"This premonition, I think the Americans call it a flashback, the fact that just before dying, people see their entire life flashing in front of them for a few seconds . . . My own flashback is slower; it has lasted this whole past year, and all of it has to do with women, but it's still a flashback . . . And once you have a flashback, you're dying, no?

"The second premonition? I'm not forgetting. I'm just not sure you want to listen to my stories anymore . . .

"The second premonition is like this. Mine is a terminal disease, but since we discovered it early enough, I can still recover completely, but I don't care that much, I don't feel the will to fight death, like the night I was struck with a lover's seizure on the sampan . . .

"Partly it's because everything is so clean . . . You're a writer, I'm sure you understand what I'm saying . . . All of a sudden, people treat me so cleanly . . .

"Before you came in, I pinched the nurse's ass, that blue-eyed, blond-haired nurse, Kelly . . .

"What're you so alarmed about? What's a little pinch on the ass? It's not going to kill anyone. I didn't pinch so that it hurts, just so it becomes an issue. Anyway, there's a part you ought to be alarmed about, I haven't gotten there yet, you're so quick . . .

"What's important was that I expected her to scream, to shout at me, or even to slap my face . . . But no, all she did was to give me this severe expression and tell me what I did was against the rules of the hospital. She dealt with my action in the same mindless way she goes about her other business, correcting me in the same mindless way she might fix the machine pumping salt water into my body . . .

"Relatives aren't any better . . . Just before she left, your aunt tried to reassure me by saying the operation will be a success . . . Not a word of complaint about my past mistakes, about my gambling habits, my affairs, my dallying with the maid, all those things, true or imagined because of jealousy, things that just a few years ago, she was still reproaching me with . . .

"Sure, things that might be considered good about me, your aunt hadn't mentioned in years. But since I became ill, she doesn't even mention my bad habits . . . She acts like all these years of living together have been just as clean as the white sheet on this bed . . . As if nothing's happened . . .

"That wife of yours, Trang, is the same way, she's pretending the operation tomorrow is as simple as a kid getting a tooth out . . . I'm always a stellar father . . . And she's never suffered or lost face because of her dad . . . Not a reproach, you know . . . Her filial respect is as cold and sterile as the hospital bed.

"Tung, my dear, you understand me now, don't you? See, the problem is, everything is so clean, so clean it's like life's been purged of its spirit . . .

"I like talking to you very much. Maybe you don't agree with me, but always, you're there listening . . . On this trip, I am going to miss only you . . .

"Sit still, let me finish . . . I love you like a friend . . . When you first got engaged to Trang, I took care of things for you, so that you two would not have to suffer like I did, or like your aunt did back then . . . Many times I sent the whole family to the movies, just so you two could be free. When you got married, I had to look all over Saigon for the Double Red ginseng roots I gave Trang to take to Da Lat . . . You're Western-educated, you don't believe it, but a honeymoon without ginseng roots wouldn't be much of a honeymoon.

"You're blushing again. Actually, it's good you're blushing. You must have red blood running in your heart or you can't blush. A robot made of aluminum and steel, welding car frames twenty-four hours a day for Toyota can't possibly blush . . .

"They say when the bamboo is old, there will be bamboo shoots. To tell the truth, it's over for my generation. Sometimes it gets depressing to think that I am living in your times . . . The men are as soft as women, and the women are as cold as ice cubes . . .

"You want to go so I can rest, huh? Or have I upset you? Maybe you've had it with a dirty old man's tales?

"It is actually getting late. You go home. Go home and rest. Me too, I'll try to sleep some, get ready for the operation tomorrow . . . It's a joy to talk to you . . ."

3.

"Oh, Tung, you're here already. The operation was a success . . . Maybe I'm still too drugged up; I'm not feeling much pain.

"They just came to take the breathing tubes out. If you'd come just a bit earlier, I wouldn't have been able to talk to you, the tubes were still in my throat . . .

"What time is it, do you know? Six o'clock, already? It's amazing, the way they put me to sleep. I slept like I was dead, didn't know anything. When I woke up, I just felt my throat burning a little . . . That other time when I went on that sampan and almost died, I actually felt cold. I didn't this time. Absolutely not, as though in all those hours, I'd been neither dead nor alive. I wasn't sleeping either because if I had been sleeping, I would have dreamt . . .

"I woke up easily, so easily. Just like they said, American surgeons are truly good . . .

"But I still feel like I am going to die . . . The operation went well but I don't feel glad . . . I do not feel completely revived . . .

"The last time on the sampan . . . Oh, I remember that incredible sharp pain when she poked the hairpin into my tailbone. I remember the smell of eucalyptus, the human odor, the smell of life . . . It's so good . . . Now all there is is the smell of fabric washed clean with detergent . . .

"You remember the hospital at home, don't you? The smell of cresyl, of iodine, each time you visit someone in the hospital, it gets soaked into your skin; your clothes would smell like the hospital for days . . . Things had scent and taste in my youth . . .

"I thank you, very much. It's because you're a writer, I can talk to you about these things . . . Others wouldn't listen at all . . .

"Don't worry, when I feel tired, when I need to rest, I'll let you know . . . I want to ask you something . . . You think I shamed my wife, huh? I wasn't decent to her, huh?

"I wasn't decent about that stuff, huh? All that stuff, like the thing about riding a horse . . . Anyway, let's forget it; you haven't opened your mouth, I already know what you want to say . . . You're just like that wife of yours, always giving me that sensitivity stuff . . . I'm pretty ridiculous too, old as I am and still asking kids about things I know all too well already anyway . . .

"But I have one favor to ask of you . . .

"You're a doctor, you're a gerontologist, you have many occasions to help me. Please look for Luyen for me . . . The other day, at the Elderly Association, I heard that she ended up marrying a Japanese man, now her husband has died, she's moved to California, but I don't know where . . . Luyen is about my age, or maybe five or seven years older in fact, but now, between seventy-one and seventy-five, seventy-six, the difference isn't all that big of a deal. I'm sure that if she hears of your reputation as a gerontologist, she'll come to see you . . .

"Do I have a photo of her? Don't be ridiculous . . . Who's gonna give a souvenir photo after a night on a sampan? I can't even remember her face . . . And even if I did remember, it'd be of no use. Who doesn't change in half a century?

"But she has a scar in the shape of a star with eight points . . . the two top parts shorter . . . The scar is right on the nine o'clock position, on her right breast; the Legionnaire who burnt her with a cigarette was left-handed . . .

"Perhaps she's wrongly accused, you know. Maybe when she was folding my clothes, the wallet had already fallen out . . . She might have found it and picked it up. Perhaps she gave in to temptation and kept it, perhaps she hadn't had a chance to return it and I already went to the police . . .

"What a pity, that bowl of chicken soup . . . It wasn't until later that I found out the prostitutes on the Perfume River believed in eating chicken soup right after they've turned a trick as a tonic, to recover the lost female energy . . . And to think that she gave up her portion for me so I could regain my strength . . .

"It would be like looking for a needle in a haystack, but if you run into her, do whatever you can to help her, for me . . . I've set aside some of my savings, I put it in the bottom of my drawer . . . Trang knows where . . . And if she doesn't want to take money, make sure she accepts my gratitude . . . You tell her that I am very sorry I reported her to the police . . .

"You say I'm a romantic . . . Romantic, my ass, I'm not that silly.

"But you're not talking about that? All right, you don't have to say anything more. You don't even have to exhale before I know what you're thinking. You're picking on me because I said 'gratitude,' right? You're thinking it's time I set my priorities straight, that a word like 'gratitude' should be reserved for your aunt. I read your black heart, didn't I?

"You writers can split a hair into four pieces . . . Of course, there's no attachment from sleeping on a sampan. It's just that I got on a roll yesterday and remembered an old story. When I babble on like that I don't always choose the right words. But you must admit I've always tried to be fair to everyone . . . That's all . . .

"Wow, now the larvae is wiser than the insect. What are you saying? My heart is pure, nonetheless, it's only my mouth that's evil? Do you really feel that way, or are you just trying to console me? What did you say? Karma? When did you become a Buddhist? You're still talking good and evil with me, even at this time? Why don't you go ahead and talk about 'redemption'?

"Enough said between uncle and nephew . . .

"Let me be. I'm just closing my eye to rest, don't worry.

"But this air conditioner is on full blast. Don't you feel cold?

"You're not shaking? I am so cold. I'm cold from way inside . . . Like there are tiny ice cubes traveling in my veins . . . Give me another blanket, they keep extra ones in that closet, in the corner of the room, over there . . .

"What . . . Why are you so agitated?

"Why did you ring the bell for the nurse? The hospital attendants are all around my bed now, this one rushing to turn on this machine, that one rushing to turn on that machine, so much clamor and confusion . . .

"What is this?

"Get rid of them for me, please. I'm chasing them out, but none of them is listening to me . . .

"Why are you crying? What kind of man are you, so ready with tears?

"You speak good English, why don't you help me send them away?

"These hospital attendants are so rude. This is my private room yet they're treating it like it's empty. They're crowding around my bed . . .

"Who's the old man on my bed? He's in a coma, his chest is bandaged all over. They're giving him shots, they're breathing into his mouth, they're pushing the breathing machine over to him . . . They're pumping electricity into his body . . . They are pushing the button; he's shocked, bending his body upward like someone with dengue fever; now he's throwing himself back down . . . It's like an emergency room scene in an American movie . . . Someone is shining a light into his eyes and shaking his head . . .

"But the patient looks so familiar, like I've seen him every day but I'm not sure where . . .

"Damn, he's me . . .

"Tung, my dear, they're pulling a blanket over my face . . .

"The American hospital blanket doesn't smell of anything. I can't even smell the detergent on it . . . Heaven, if only I had Luyen's blanket . . . I want it so badly; if I can just smell the eucalyptus, the odor of sweat, the saliva, Luyen's odor . . . Oh, the odor of life . . .

"But listen to me carefully . . .

"I don't have much time left . . .

"Try to find Luyen for me . . .

"Luyen with the scar on the right breast, around the nine o'clock position . . .

"Because the Legionnaire was left-handed . . ."

Translated by Nguyen Qui Duc

GUNBOAT ON THE YANGTZE

Tran Vu

One day Toan comes up behind me, covers my head with a black veil and says: "Sometimes you can see through a blindfold."

And with these enigmatic words, he leaves. I turn around. The veil wriggles, snaking around his hand. Like a dance.

"It's the invisible that really exists."

Words. Always incomprehensible, ambiguous. The veil writhes, opens into a fan, palpitates like a bat's wing, slithering and bending like a dead snake. A kind of cobra. A flash shoots through my mind. I see a cobra poised, ready to attack. Toan approaches, flicking the veil, skillfully, like a matador. He folds it into a blindfold and pulls it over my eyes.

"What do you see, Elder Sister?"

His face is so close I can feel the heat of his breathing.

"I see nothing."

Violently, he pulls the blindfold tighter. "Can you see now?"

I shake my head. He pulls it tighter. My eyes burn.

"It's only when we're in pain that we take the trouble to think."

He yanks the ends of the blindfold. I can't see him, but I feel the sweat from his wrists against my face, imagine his arm muscles flexing. The blindfold tightens, crushing my temples.

"That's enough!"

My cry dissipates the humid, suffocating atmosphere of the room. Toan goes out. Groping, I undo the blindfold, hang it on the back of a chair. A snake's corpse. My eyes still smart. Toan has slunk into a corner. He plays his favorite tune on the cello. The music resonates, note by note, phrase by phrase, scale by scale, by turns grave, strident, haunting.

Toan is seated, his head slightly bowed. He looks at me with his formless eyes, pulls fervently at the bow. He wraps his left arm around the body of the cello, passionately, like a man would embrace a woman. The bow advances, retreats, relentless. The cello squeaks like an old saw scraping a piece of iron wire. A murky, wrenching, tortured sound that slowly permeates the room, engulfing the library, the table, crawling toward me.

"That's enough!"

I shout again. I can't stand his obstinate, deformed gaze. Abruptly the cello falls silent. The bow slides off the strings. Round and voluptuous, the body of the cello is like a woman's.

"Are you forbidding me to play, or to look at you?" Toan snaps.

"Both."

"That's right. We're only stones, inert stones."

He snickers and disappears into his room.

I stay there, alone, anxious.

Toan has lived in his own strange world, haunted by these shadows, for a long time. Tonight, the strangeness seems to have grown. What's worse, I know why. I wipe the clammy sweat from my cheek that, for all this time, has been seeping into my skin. I go into my room. Toan thrashes around in his. I pull the covers over my head, trying to block out the spasms of a body tortured by loneliness. But from under the blankets, in the darkness that engulfs me, I see it again: the night Toan wanted to make me see.

* * *

Daylight came, I woke up late, disoriented. I hadn't slept at all, had just lain there on my back, staring at the black veil, holding my head in my hands. It was a bleak morning. Toan's silhouette is engraved in my door frame. Outside, bony, skeleton-like trees strained their thin arms toward the sky, as if to ask for divine grace. I move toward the dining room table for my breakfast: coffee, one sugar cube. At home, Toan always takes care of breakfast. Every morning he puts the sugar cube next to my coffee cup. I understand.

"You told me you would never leave me, that you would live for me alone. Do you remember?" he says, detecting my presence.

"I remember."

"So, what are you waiting for? Who sacrificed himself for you?"

"I know, *you* did." I respond mechanically, unable to look him in the face. Gently he approaches, behind my back, like he did the night before, and plasters his hands over my eyes.

"Stop!"

I struggle to free myself, from his fingers, from the night. He pants. A heavy, staggered breathing.

His fingers slowly relax, press my temples, fondle my cheek, brush against my chin, massage my neck. I shudder; his hands grip me like tentacles. He keeps pummeling me, sometimes violent, sometimes caressing. I shudder and shove him away.

"That's enough. Stop!"

"That's enough. That's all you can say."

He turns me around, runs his finger down the bridge of my nose to my lips. I yield, accept his games. Why? So he won't destroy himself from despair.

Suddenly, his face falls. The scar across his lip deepens. Panicked, I throw my arms on his chest, spill his cup of coffee

on me, over the couch. He grabs my face, draws me toward
his lips.

"You've seen movies. You must know how to kiss."

"That's enough!"

He offers me his shredded lips, and as I turn away, they fall
onto my cheek, at once dry and clammy. His mouth sticks to
my cheek, he burrows his head in the curve of my neck,
refuses to pull back. I don't resist anymore. My body soaked
with coffee, I hug him to me. When I touch his shattered face,
the puffy ridges of skin between the gashes, I feel no horror. I
love him, pity him.

"That's enough now. Go play the cello."

He looks at me, indifferent, distant, like he does every time
I refuse. But he seems to have softened. Now the cello again,
like yesterday evening, grave, distraught, anarchic. Who
knows what he hears in this music that he plays day in and
day out, month after month. I don't . . . But I know he wants
me to see through the blindfold.

"You need a girlfriend," I tell him, when he least expects
it, as he is bent over his cello. The cello abruptly falls silent. His
misshapen eyes lift toward me.

"What did you say?"

"You need a girlfriend."

"Who would dare love me?"

"I'll find her for you."

After a long silence, he gets up, moves toward the window,
opens it. Wind rushes into the room. The curtains rise and
fall, flapping, palpitating like butterfly wings impaled on a pin.
Toan turns toward me, deliberately exposing his ravaged face,
the scars I have watched go white under the botched sutures,
that I have seen crust over under the burning sun of the
islands. In the light of day, his exploded face is horrible.

"Take a good look, Elder Sister. Who could love this face? Do
you think I don't know what my face is like? All I have to do is
touch it."

He puts his hand to his own face, his fingers suddenly

arch, his nails clawing into the flesh, as if to rip away its hideous shape.

"Toan! Stop it!" I scream, throwing myself onto him, grabbing the fingers that dig into his face. His body tenses, his back arching as if he wants to flee. He lets out a long, painful cry. I press my face to his, hug his head to my shoulder, massage his rough skin, stroke his scars.

"Don't do that anymore, Toan. Never again, you hear me? Never again."

"You don't love me."

"I can't. I don't have the right to . . ."

He hugs me. I wait until he calms down, and then gently pry open his arms. "I'll find you a friend, I swear it." I say this, exhausted.

He goes into the kitchen, picks up a book, as if he wanted to overcome his emotion. His fingers grope over the Braille, letter by letter, word by word, searching for meaning on this piece of paper. It kills me to watch. Nothing is more painful than watching someone you love dying from the inside, slowly. My friends' faces file past my eyes, dissolving in questions, hesitation, doubt, fear. Joelle, Kate, Florence, Isabelle? Any woman will do. As long as it's not me. It will never be me.

* * *

Kate comes in, takes off her coat and hat. Her auburn hair tumbles down the line of buttons on the front of her wool sweater. As she settles on the couch, she tells me not to go to any trouble. She glances around. I know who she wants to see. "Would you like something to drink?" I ask, knowing she never does. As expected, she shakes her head. I insist. She accepts. I pour her a glass of vodka and stare at the transparent liquid while she drinks, as if to steel her courage.

"It's good when it's cold out."

Kate sets the glass on the table, rubs her hands, relaxed now. She's still young, probably the same age as Toan, but she seems very mature. Seeing her so calm, so relaxed, calms me. I speak to her about Toan, tell her that he's had an accident, that he's forced to live like a recluse, how miserable he is, and that if she could come see him now and then, maybe on weekends, sometimes . . .

Kate asks me a few vague questions about his life, if he likes music, books. We have so many books in the apartment. I tell her that Toan likes to play the cello, that the library is mine, that Toan can only read a few books, the kind written for people like him. She is surprised, asks why. I try to explain that Toan doesn't see clearly, that he has been wounded in the eyes. I want to prepare her, but she seems so sure of herself, tells me again not to worry.

"I understand. I know about these things. Don't worry. I'm sure we'll be friends." She takes my arm, encouragingly. She seems relaxed, calm. Just then, Toan's cello echoes through the room. Kate's flinches, her face changes. I understand; Toan's formless, distraught tune is so familiar, but each time I hear it, even I find it eerie, chilling.

Still, Kate gets up and asks to see him. I walk her to Toan's room. I knock on the door, introduce a friend. He doesn't answer. The cello grates out the same tune. I push the door open. Toan is seated, his back turned to us. His shoulders heave in time with the cello, his arms following the to and fro of the bow. I hear Kate say hello, watch her as she enters his room. Toan keeps playing, his head bent over the cello, as if he had heard nothing. Kate stands behind him. I watch Toan, listening to the music eddy around the room. Suddenly, I am furious, jealous. I regret having brought Kate here. The thought that I am going to lose Toan saddens me. Kate places her hands on Toan's shoulders.

No one expected what happened. Not me, not Kate, not even him. Toan slowly turned his head, exposing his ravaged, shriveled flesh, the two holes that masquerade as his eyes, his deformed half-nose, the long gash that cuts across his forehead, through his lips, all the way down to his chin. Kate's features froze, and she let out a scream of terror. Her cry paralyzed me. She ran out, calling for help. Her scream haunted that corridor for a long time. Toan's cello lay on the floor. Tears streamed from the sockets of his eyes, the gnarled flesh of his face was wet with pain and shame. He sobbed in silence. I wept too, and hugged his head to me violently, my tears mingling with his, falling into those sockets.

"No one can love me, no one can be my friend," he moaned.

I put my hand over his mouth and tell him I love him, that I will be the friend, that I will rescue him from his solitude, help him live the normal life of a normal young man, that I'll do everything to, anything to . . . He asks me what I am protecting, what it is that I regret. And I tell him everything, how I have nothing more to protect, that I was raped at sea, that I won't refuse him any longer.

We coil around each other on the floor. He nuzzles his head in my hair, weeping silently. I pat his shoulder like I used to, to console him. That was such a long time ago. Old memories, of our childhood, of that sisterly love rise in me, rekindling sweet images of the past. Toan and I are one, the same blood flows in our veins. That I will give myself to him now won't change much, we will only be mingling our common blood. I won't ever belong to another man, can't, no matter who he might be. All men horrify me, except for Toan. We gaze at the clouds, as they glide silent and serene across the windowpane. I describe them to Toan, the colors, how the horizon fades in the distance. Entwined like this, we share the same shadows. A kiss, long, penetrating, like the night. Now we no longer belong to the moral, human world.

* * *

The first night we dine in silence. He is seated facing me, his head bent over, carefully rotating his bowl of rice. It is raining. Drops of water splash all around. From the ceiling, the lamp casts a dim, cloudy light over the table. I watch it dapple his face with tiny patches, forcing myself not to see the scars, to imagine the light flowering into golden blooms. He eats laboriously. We both wait for someone to speak. Toan's hand slips under the table, searching for mine. Our fingers open, cross, our hands throbbing with emotion, with desire. Toan stays silent, his head bowed, but I hear him through his touching. After dinner, he takes me to his room.

We stand side by side in the shadows. The light from the street lamp, outside, refracted in the rain, illuminates the room, scattering into glistening shards on Toan's back. I let him undress me. His hands, like a blind person's, are nimble, intelligent. He undoes the buttons one by one, places his lips on my flesh with each measure that he frees it. As he lifts off my bra, lightning flashes through the room, exposing his face. I shudder, glimpsing in the electric blue flash another kind of light, cold, and metallic, the blinding blows of a machete. And other machetes spring forth, thunder down, lacerate, hacking away at Toan's face. Through the lightning flashes, I see a tempest, my own convulsed body fading and reappearing, shattered images engraved on the warped screen of Toan's face.

"No."

I pull back, terrified.

Sensing my confusion, he draws me into his arms, sending the warmth of his body through mine. He whispers love in my ear, infinite love. "I love you. I don't regret anything. Don't look at my face, or you'll be frightened."

He tells me to turn around, to not be afraid anymore, to forget, not to think anymore, to live for us, only us, just him and me. I yield, promise to forget . . . He comes closer, encircling me in his arms, pressing his body down on my back. The patter of rain against the windowpane, Toan's tender, murmuring voice asking if he can enter me from behind, my own voice telling him yes, I need him, belong to him. And then all that is left here, in the apartment, are two beings who love each other.

The other day, when he blindfolded me with the black veil, the warmth of his body penetrated me, swirling inside me. Through the black veil, I saw us clearly, our two naked bodies merged, Toan's arms clasped at my waist, his lips caressing my neck, my shoulders, the bite of his teeth on my back. Welling up from the deepest part of my being, a long, shuddering tenderness rises and spreads through my body. Covered by the gift of this fraternal love, in the slow, attentive rocking of his body, the pain, the wounds of the past melt into a startling happiness.

We loved each other in the shadows, in the healing tenderness of caresses that effaced the unhappiness of our past. Toan led me to bed, and I sobbed on his shoulder, consoled, freed. My tears spilt over, burning, on his chest. He fondled my chin, asked me if I loved him, if I was happy, if I regretted this. And I told him that I loved him, that I was happy, that I didn't regret anything. No doubt this was sin, but who would ever understand me, know the price of a drop of fraternal blood in the ocean of life, feel how much I needed Toan, this drop of my own blood?

The moon rose. The rain stopped. We lay next to each other, listening to the silence, the primal night of our origins, lost somewhere in the prehistory of mankind. Once, in the tribes, a brother and sister could marry. Toan and I, we were just restoring life to what it had once been, at the dawn of mankind. The emptiness of the night shielded me from the gaze of others, from morality. In this night, we were all that existed, a brother and sister who loved each other.

* * *

The days that followed, the first of our life together, were wonderful. I was everything for Toan: elder and younger sister, lover, wife. And he was all for me, at once little brother, lover, husband. What awe one feels when feelings merge, when one loves. I suffered when he was absent. Hours spent at the office weighed on me, heavy with longing. I would run home to press myself to him, to melt in his arms. Impatient kisses, passionate embraces. At night, on my pillow, Toan would speak of the past.

"Remember our walks, at night, on the beach behind Vũng Tàu? I still remember your violet *ao dai* on the yellow sand, the way the beach stretched all the way to the mountains. Back then, your hair came all the way down your back, and the wind kept time with the clouds. I've loved you ever since. Did you know?"

Did you know? His face in my hair, he murmurs to me, rubs his nose on the nape of my neck. In these moments, we relive the past, a time when he still had a nose, when I still had the long hair of an adolescent who hasn't yet been drowned in shame. And Toan stirred many other memories in me, as if, blind to the present and the future, his eyes could only see the ancient images of the past.

"Remember the first time you put on makeup? For Thuan's birthday party? Niem brought over face powder. I hid behind the door. Maybe you didn't know it. That night, papa locked you in your room, forbade you to go out. You cried all night. That made me cry too, remember?"

Remember? Yes, I remember. How he had always been at my back, how he had demanded affection, followed me like a shadow, never leaving me for a second. How he used to refuse to sleep alone, how he sulked whenever Thuan went on walks with me.

"You still love him, don't you? He kissed you, didn't he? What else did he do with you?"

Jealous, bitter, he often plied me with questions. If I answered, he would be furious, making love to me violently, clawing my back with his nails, as if to take revenge. Afterward he would weep and beg me to forgive him. If I shook my head, insisting that Thuan was just a friend, he would be reassured that I only belonged to him, as he wished it.

"Swear to me. That you'll be with no one but me."

And I would swear, knowing that I could never leave him, never live apart from him.

We hugged each other, took refuge in the common warmth of our bodies. Outside the snow fell in drifts. Snowflakes gathered on the windowsill, freezing and melting, and freezing again. All winter we hid ourselves in the apartment, avoided the world. I feared our love would be discovered; Toan feared I would abandon him. We could sleep together for hours and hours on end, engulfed in the warmth of the covers.

Between embraces, after I had offered myself to him, I would see it floating on the ceiling. The word. *"Incest."* I would hide my head in his shoulder, fleeing this invisible word that was nevertheless writ large and clear on the ceiling.

A black veil over the eyes is the best way for me to stop seeing it. Sometimes, on the weekends, I kept it on all day, sharing Toan's world without light. We played hide-and-seek in the apartment. Hidden behind a door, an armoire, we held our breath . . . Toan gave me my first lessons in this world of the blind. How do you walk in the dark? How many steps between the kitchen and the living room? How many arm lengths between the table and the television? How do you know when food is cooked?

"By tasting it!"

He burst out laughing when I asked him that question.

"If you want to keep track of time, know whether it is day or night, you have to learn how to keep track of your own hunger, digestion."

"But how do you choose exactly which clothes to wear?"

"You must learn to feel the fabric, to give a scent to each article of clothing . . ."

Little by little, I learned, entering with delight into this shadowy world. Every time I tripped, he burst out laughing. Whenever he confused wheat flour with corn flour, I giggled, mocking him. I had begun to grasp these brief moments of happiness, had begun to understand them, to share them with Toan, ever since we had become husband and wife.

I had never known such happiness. The happiness of being a normal woman, of living with a man. It was a kind of happiness that, ever since the event, I thought I had lost forever. Toan began to attend a school for the blind, and he brought work home to help me out financially. Miserable as the work was, the extra money was a joy for us. Toan was happy; he felt useful. I was happy to see him lead a less abnormal life, to see him work at his cello playing, to see him studying French in Braille. He gave up drinking and smoking. This moved me; I realized that he was trying to become a model husband. Sometimes he would stammer like a child, trying to avoid the word . . . Elder Sister.

"Do you still love me?"

"Always. But only if you still call me Elder Sister."

"Why won't you let me call you by your name?"

"I love you, so I always want to be your Elder Sister, understand?"

He would acquiesce and fall silent, let me stroke the locks of hair across his forehead. Sometimes, on moonlit nights, we went for walks. Each time, I would dress up and carefully apply my makeup, so he would know I had made myself beautiful for him, so that he would be proud to walk by my side.

Being sensitive, he would wait for me. When he knew I was finished, he would tell me, with a serious air, how beautiful I was, and gaze at me passionately. These moments hurt me; when his finger touched my lips to search for their color, when he had to feel the fabric of my clothes to guess what I was wearing.

"You're beautiful tonight. I'm proud of you."

At these moments, I felt like crying, but I controlled my feelings, so as not to ruin the evening. I adjusted his tie, and we would go out. Usually Toan took my hand, slipped it in his coat pocket. We took deserted back alleys, so that Toan wouldn't hear the murmurs of passersby, the children's frightened shrieks. We knew a restaurant near us. We only dared go on Mondays, when it was nearly deserted. The old restaurant owner reserved a table for me in a corner, with a candle and a rose.

"Don't order anything expensive. I only want to be here with you, the food doesn't matter."

We dined in the tender candlelight, the rose slowly opened, the old man was attentive.

"Did you like the meal?"

"Oh yes, it was perfect."

Toan answered for me, uninhibited, happy, contented. Under the table, the whole meal long, our legs were entwined.

* * *

Winter ends in the secrecy of our love. Spring. Outside, in the streets, chestnut trees are covered with yellow shoots, their sinuous branches outstretched like the arms of young girls, weaving crowns of flowers and fruit. Green shoots pry forth in search of life. For a moment, in this flickering light, in this wonder of natural beauty, I am reborn. I fall back to earth when Toan asks me for a child . . .

I refuse, horrified. The idea of having a child with Toan pierces me, spilling the blood of our sin. The thought of it rips away the black veil I had used to hide from our incestuous love. I ask Toan: What would we say to our parents, to our family, to our relatives? We can't live in seclusion, in hiding, for our whole life. Children conceived in incest are often abnormal.

I am terrified. Every time he mentions his desire to have a child, I tremble.

"Don't think about that anymore. Never think about that. I'm afraid."

Toan moans, begs, grabs me violently by the waist.

"Give me a child, just a child. He'll call us papa, mama. We'll give him so much love."

Night after night, he begs me, insistent, distraught, oblivious to the incestuousness of our love. I have bent my mind to love him, but I don't have the courage to give our crime a human shape. How would we explain our relationship to the child, the relationship between its parents?

And I cry when he covers my neck with kisses.

"But I want one, I want one!"

And he shakes his head, stubborn, selfish. I cry, in vain, bitter.

Toan doesn't understand, doesn't realize that I have reached the extreme limits of an elder sister's love. He just thinks I am rejecting him. His attitude toward me changes, he retreats into his shadowy silence, into his old violence. Slowly, imperceptibly, he is transformed, becomes domineering, imperious, mean. He forbids me to take my pill. Obsessed with the desire to force me to have a child with him, he searches the apartment, uncovers all my hiding places. At night, I don't dare sleep with him anymore. During the day, I drown myself in the television so as to avoid all conversation. I feel constantly spied upon. I live on the defensive, expecting his attacks at any moment.

* * *

The night it happened, I was watching an old film. Disparate images paraded past my eyes, taking shape, dissolving. Toan's cello whined again; it had taken on its old, tuneless voice, unfeeling, soulless, and it wrapped around my brain like barbed wire, penetrating with hammer-like thuds. I could hear this shrill, razor-sharp sound, like a sliver of glass ripping through flesh, while on the screen I watched the turbulent story. I remember the French title of the film: *Gunboat on the Yangtze*. Steve McQueen played a sailor on an American warship in China that ferried soldiers between Hankou and Hangzhou. There were horrible, dramatic moments, terrifying psychological revelations, incidents of abnormal, instinctive behavior. That's all I remember. The rest, the other images, weren't of the film, but of a fetus growing in its mother's body. I saw it on the screen, the placenta bursting, the umbilical cord sagging, the syringes, a white body that pushed and pushed, blood gushing. And in the surge of blood, a tiny, pointed skull that drew back, reluctant. In the middle of the exploded, bloody uterus, I saw a baby's skull with Steve McQueen's face, lips twisted, eyes rolled back, just like at the end of the film, when the actor falls, struck by a bullet, and then raises himself to his feet, staggering, then crawling, through the sticky liquid. His terrified, distraught eyes fix on the hole in his stomach where the blood gushes from. I hear the last words of a dying man. "But, but . . . My God! What has happened to me! Yesterday I was still at home!" The child struggled, scratched, kicking the air with its legs. The mother's uterus splits open, the mad screech of the cello grates on my raw, anesthetized nerves. Sounds and images jumble, couple, merge and superimpose in my head. On the screen, I can't understand the sailor's words. I want to understand, want to see the child's real face, but now, after the flood, the cello falls silent. No more music, no more sounds of glass, of smashed bottles, of a door slamming, of blood ebbing away, of a heart that ceases to beat, of lungs that stop breathing, of a uterus closing. Toan stands behind me, motionless.

"Give me a child."

"No, I can't."

He isn't listening. In a blue flash, he brandishes a razor blade against my face. Suddenly, he slices a cello string. One. He groans. He picks up the razor blade again, waving it in the air like the black veil, uncertain. The vision of a snake's body coiling around my neck comes back to me as Toan presses the blade to my neck and, gently, cuts. I feel the heat of my own blood flowing. Paralyzed, terrified, I struggle, my hands shake wildly.

"Stop!"

"You don't love me."

"But I do."

"That's a lie. If you love me, why do you refuse to have my child?"

He screams. He cuts another cello string. Two.

"No! Please, don't force me to do it."

I push him away, push him over and flee. He pursues me. The books, the table, the stools—everything topples under me. I fall flat on my face, pull myself up, fall again, the flowerpot trips me, the door blocks my way, now down the long, endless corridor. The bathroom, the bathroom, the lock, my father's name, my mother's name, I shout them in answer to Toan's furious blows against the door.

"For God's sake, spare me."

Toan doesn't hear me. He pushes down the door and jumps on me, tears off my shirt.

"No! Let go of me!"

I fall onto the tile floor. Toan falls on top of me. *I am handicapped. I'm somewhere between madness and sanity. Is that what scares you? Is that it? You're afraid the child will look like me, is that it? Say it!* He slaps me, tears away my shirt, my hands. His fingers twist my arm, his thighs crush my legs, he pants and shouts, the floor, the walls, the ceiling, the towels, naked, clammy bodies, strong shoulders, muscles tensed, a brute force that bites, scratches, pierces, the nose, those eyes, the scars, the sperm, the fetus, the child, I cry for my mother. Toan gags me, smothering my voice with his hand.

"Say it! Say that you love me, that you want my child. Say it! Say it!"

Toan raped me on the bathroom floor. He said he was hungry for my sweet-smelling flesh, for my firm breasts, my fresh, white thighs, for a child, a lively handsome one. He talked on and on, without stopping, while I thrashed and sobbed and shouted and supplicated, while I suffered.

I lay naked on the floor, lay there in the bathroom turned on end, my senses scattered, haunted by an idea that I couldn't articulate, feeling blood trickle down my lip. All of a sudden the film came back to me, slowly and clearly. I just lay there, seeing the film again. The fight between the sailor and his comrades. The captain's moral struggle. The fanatical Chinese. The violence. The assistant mechanic being tortured. The young, naive evangelist. The bullet that shot through Steve McQueen's stomach, the words gushing forth at the end, near death. What were the words? What did he mean? I couldn't understand them. It was as if I were watching a silent film.

After a long time, I get up. It is daylight out. Toan is slumped over the dining room table, sobbing. Slow, innocent moans. He cries like he did as a child. The window is ajar. There's no sun out. I gaze at the murky, clouded sky.

All at once I remember everything, each detail, with precision. The moment I got on the boat to leave my country, the pirates' attacks, everything up to the moment that Toan raped me . . .

I remember the final words of the wounded sailor. *But, but . . . My God, what happened? Yesterday, we were still at Vũng Tàu!* I collapse. Toan turns his ravaged face toward me. Scars. My God, it's daylight.

Translated by Nina McPherson and Phan Huy Duong

THE PRE-WAR ATMOSPHERE

Do Khiem

*H*e comes home. The blue light on the answering machine flickers silently, a message from his wife: "I'm drinking with friends at the Olive Garden in Brea. Do you want to come down for dinner? It's 6:30. I'll call back in a bit." "Brea" in Arabic means "empty valley," but is transformed in Spanish into "tar." The southern Californians in Orange County are a tolerant bunch. When he arrived, the county was still undeveloped: orange groves, oil rigs, yellow grass. But there were bulldozers everywhere, paving new streets. Okay, so a word can mean both empty valley and tar. The titters behind his wife's voice on the answering machine put him in a festive mood. He goes into his room to change.

By the time she calls back, he is dressed up and rereading a few pages of Raymond Chandler's *The Long Goodbye*. Philip Marlowe is drinking a gimlet at Victor's.

"I was living that year in a house on Yucca Avenue in the Laurel Canyon district. It was a small hillside house on a dead-end street with a long flight of redwood steps to the front door and a grove of eucalyptus trees across the way."

A gimlet is half gin, half lime juice, with a few drops of angostura and syrup. He asks his wife:

"What you drinking?"

"I'm drinking a Bloody Mary. You coming to eat? My friends want to leave."

"Do you know how to mix a gimlet?"

"No."

"Do they have gimlets there?"

"How would I know?" His wife, noticing his roundaboutness, suggests, "All right, I'll come pick you up. Do you want to eat Japanese?"

Why Japanese? he thinks.

His wife says:

"You think about it. Wait for me."

His wife shows up, thinking he knows not what. Marlowe is easy: The man's loyal to one drink, at least for a story.

"From then on it got to be a habit with him to drop in around 5 o'clock. We didn't always go to the same bar, but oftener to Victor's than anywhere else."

Without knowing why, he demands:

"I want to eat Lebanese."

"You want to eat and watch the belly dancer?" His wife asks.

"Belly dancing?"

"Hassan in Newport Beach. All my friends say it's a good place to eat."

"Which friends, American or Lebanese?"

"American."

He looks at his wife.

"American friends, I wouldn't trust them."

His wife agrees.

He continues:

"You're Lebanese but you let Americans tell you where to eat your own food."

His wife shrugs. Unlike the Vietnamese, the Lebanese are not passionately attached to their homeland. They don't have a beef soup to haunt them—raw or well-done with its clear broth, a peeled onion, a raw egg. Perhaps his wife is unusually indifferent. There were times, watching the news on TV, when he would say, "Hey, there's fighting in Beirut," and his wife would respond, "Oh, really?" Maybe this is why the Lebanese have assimilated quickly and gained powerful positions in their adopted countries. Philip Habib as Special Envoy, for example, or John Sununu as White House Chief of Staff. Not to mention someone whose name he can't remember who is president of a small country in the Caribbean.

"I don't like to watch belly dancing." He could conjure up scenes from Egyptian movies, "They jiggle their bellies right at your table. It makes me uncomfortable."

His wife laughs:

"You are uncomfortable with everything. It's Friday night, there's belly dancing everywhere, including Indian restaurants."

Belly dancing even in Indian restaurants, all because it is such a popular feature in America, a kind of aerobics, with appeal for Americans, not Indians.

He says:

"That's all right. I want to eat Lebanese."

The Gondole restaurant is on Lincoln between Dale and Beach, which is closer to where he lives than Newport Beach. "I've never noticed it. Did you bring the address?" His wife slows down the car.

"2700 or 2800 West."

He vaguely remembers, looking right and left at all the signs shining on the dark street. A gas station, fried chicken, an apartment complex, pizza, waterbeds, Indian grocery store ("How come so many Indians are named Patel?" he wonders), a mobile home park ("Now Renting"), a sushi restaurant, and a California Sun Tan outlet.

"Here, on this side," he points.

Gondole Club/Restaurant.

The strip mall's architecture has the feel of a New England town; its bell tower resembles the spire of a small-town church. The wooden wall has turned blue under the neon light. The parking lot is empty, dark, cozy, except for a dimly lit "For Lease" sign. This complex is relatively new. The two cloth screens shielding the entrance to the sushi place flutter. California Sun Tan, right next door, must be hurting for business. April's temperature has unexpectedly reached the record-breaking 100s. One could go mad sitting in a car: Who would want to go into a salon and lie under a Light Bulb Beach?

The Gondole Restaurant claims the end spot. He has to look carefully at the image on the glass to detect a sinuous woman holding a scarf above her head. First the spire, now the stained glass. "Gondole" is spelled out in big letters. Driving by, he used to think it was an Italian restaurant. And the image of the dancing woman he had mistaken for a gondolier: a guy in a black hat singing bel canto in front of San Marco, not a belly dancer untying the scarf around her stomach to flutter over her head. Why would an Arabic eatery be called "Gondole"? He notices the small letters, "Lebanese Cuisine," on the side wall and the Arabic script over the door.

"What does that say?" he asks his wife.

"*Al Gondole.*"

"Oh."

The name makes sense if you think about it. Venice is part of the East. Actually, the East begins in Venice. Beirut is right on the other side, the next stop on the spice route. It is both the entry to the Arabic peninsula and the gateway to Europe. Separated by a bit of tranquil sea, the Mediterranean, Europeans who come to Venice already feel they are entering the East. On both ends are doors, with the Mediterranean a nondescript and neutral hallway. So an Arabic eatery in Orange County, the new Byzantium, can be called "Al Gondole." There's nothing irrational about it.

They enter.

He sees, from afar, the promised belly dancer. "Wednesday to Saturday, belly dancing with live Arabic music." A young waiter, tall, with an actor's good looks, leads them to the end of the room. On a platform hugging the wall is a long row of couches, arranged in several Us. Each has a table at a height about halfway between a dining room table and a coffee table. They settle down, half sitting, half lying. The rest of the row is already filled with diners. Beneath where they're sitting, the regular tables and chairs are unoccupied. At the back, in front of a shimmering, multicolored, gold-threaded curtain, is a blond dancer in a Haroun el Rashid harem costume. He leans back and stares at the soft ceiling, made of silk or brocade to resemble the tent roof of a nomadic sheik—very clever, but there's no atmosphere yet, in spite of the dancer's exertion at the back of the room.

"This ceiling reminds me of the Indian restaurant," he tells his wife.

The Indian restaurant was near the ocean (everything was near the ocean in Beirut), with a cloth ceiling that resembled the interior of a tent. It was hot there also—the night before Zouheir Moshen was killed. That day, the Arabic waiter asked him which wine he preferred, French or local. Tonight he wants a Lebanese wine but cannot find one on the menu. There are only Lebanese beers, and European or American wines. Although there are many fine California wines, he doesn't have a clue about them. They had even sold them at Hediard in Paris. Eating Tex-Mex in Bastille, the fancy crowd in the City of Lights would swear by Napa Valley and Sonoma.

"You want another long drink?" he asks.

"I just drank two Bloody Mary's. A Bloody Mary at the Olive Garden is like this," his wife measures about twelve inches with her hands. "You should drink an Almaza beer."

In Beirut he only dared to drink Almaza in the cheap joints. In the Hamra district, at Express or Café de Paris, he would follow the crowd and drink Heineken. He wonders if they know how to make a gimlet here like they do at the bar at the Ritz Beverly Hotel?

The waiter returns and asks courteously:

"Would you like something to drink?"

He hesitates, flips the menu back and forth and turns to his wife several times for help. It is hopeless. Waiters are different everywhere. In France, they are solemn and attentive. In the States they're eager and in your face. This guy is Lebanese. He's got a Middle East refinement and deserves the title "maitre" (the Lebanese call a waiter "maitre," a French word, the same word the Vietnamese use for a lawyer). He glances at "Louis Fuisse, Louis Jadot, $39." He blurts out:

"Mateus Rose."

Then exhales. Oh well, Mateus Rose, a Portuguese wine. The maitre leaves. His wife looks over:

"Pouilly Fuisse," she reminds him.

"I know, 39 bucks," he replies.

He's not picky. You save 20 bucks going from Maconnais to Minho. Muscat from the Douro is a pretty good black gamay from the Saône. Yet the price is less than half. The waiter comes back, fussily shows him the bottle and lets him sniff the cork, which embarrasses him a little. A *vin de table* without a proper name and this guy is making a fuss. He tastes and nods his frugal head, like the night he drank the local wine in the Indian restaurant on the Lebanese hills. He feels love for his wife. The next night Zouheir Mohsen died.

There is no atmosphere at that point. A single belly dancer does not make the Middle East.

"This one can dance," his wife enthuses earnestly.

He turns his body halfway and awkwardly watches the blond American rhythmically flash the flesh around her belly button. At the entrance, he had carefully studied the black and white photograph without detecting anything Arabic about her other than the "Thousand and One Nights" outfit. "Her name is Chadia," he mumbles, "but I'm sure she's American."

Chadia, pausing at each table to wiggle her body, is coming near. At the next table, two American couples become rowdy and wave dollar bills in the air. One fun-loving guy is trying to insert money into her cleavage while his girlfriend, legs on the couch, laughs hysterically. Chadia evades him adroitly, "Not allowed, not allowed," but she sticks her hip out so he can tuck money into the elastic hem of her pants. The guy, bewildered, shoves the money to his girlfriend under the table so she can tip for him.

"If you think she's good, give her some money. Here she comes."

His wife laughs, "If you don't like it, turn away; she'll leave automatically. There's nothing to be afraid of."

"I don't like it," he says adamantly.

Sometimes life's more simple than you think. Chadia comes to their table, wiggles moderately a few times, then really does leave. Maintaining his sullen look, he exhales audibly.

"I know how to tip at go-go bars," he says apologetically. "A dollar is easy to figure out."

"You can tip whatever you want here. What's the difference?"

"I'm used to nude dancing. I'm not inhibited by it. This is your culture; you deal with it."

"Culture nothing. Belly dancing represents the sexual act."

Of course it's culture: human elaboration. A dog will represent the sexual act more simply, without ostentation. He goes on:

"People will belly dance at a political rally. I've seen them do it to 'Che Guevara in Gaza.' "

And he had seen it. At the Mutualite Theater in Paris, when Marcel Khalife was performing, some women in the audience left their seats, tied keffiyehs around their hips and danced in the aisles. The girl who was with him clapped along, her shoulders bobbing—a sexual act or *hasta la victoria sempre*? Since Chadia has gone to the dressing room, he feels genuinely safe. His wife says:

"Politics, sex, same difference. You can turn around now."

He turns around and notices, under the flickering oil lamp, a little sign on the table: "$15 minimum after 10 o'clock." Perhaps the main program only begins after 10 o'clock. The blonde with the Chadia moniker was only an opening act.

"I only know how to tip nude dancers," he is still embarrassed.

The sun was very hot. Big patches of his shirt stuck to his back uncomfortably.

"The stretch of broken-paved road from the highway to the curve of the hill was dancing in the noon heat . . . A thin hot acrid breeze was blowing. I had my coat off and my sleeves rolled up, but the door was too hot to rest an arm on."

His wife, hair tied behind her ears, smiled at him from the sidewalk.

"Where you going?"

His wife wasn't his wife at that point.

"I was browsing in Antoine's."

"You want to go get a drink?"

"I just had a drink with a friend."

He pointed to his Japanese friend. This guy was not really a friend. They had just had a drink. He met the guy on the street—he's Asian, the other guy's Asian—and they had a drink. He said, "You live here?" The other guy said, "No, you live here?" He said, "No." The other guy said, "I'm taking the bus to Baalbeck later. Want to come?" He said, "Yes, I was planning on taking the bus to Baalbeck."

"I'm going to Mövenpick for ice cream," his wife said.

He looked at the Japanese guy, who saw that he had met a local girl and was talking to her in French on the sidewalk—not a promising sign. Sometimes life's more simple than you think. The other guy split voluntarily.

"I'm taking the bus to Baalbeck."

"Yeah, you go," he said. "I'm going with you to Mövenpick for ice cream," he said to his wife.

His wife smiled; the Japanese guy left. This guy he would never meet again; Baalbeck he would never see; his wife is still his wife today and the ice cream in Mövenpick was nothing to talk about. His wife is still his wife and the two of them are drinking cheap Mateus Rose, eating mez and waiting for 10 o'clock to see what the next attraction is.

Most of the American patrons left after the belly dancing act that had embarrassed him. The place is filling up with Arabs. At the next table are two sisters, who appear to be waiting for somebody, each drinking a Coke and not saying much. There is no one on stage. On the cassette player is a quiet tape by Magda Al Rumi.

"This girl's young. She's of Mona Mar'achli's generation," his wife says.

"I don't know her."

The young ones he doesn't know. There are famous songs he knows the melody of, and there are some he can sing along so people can laugh. Even with his bad pronunciation and his out-of-tune voice, he still likes to sing. Nothing could be funnier than the time they returned to Beirut. His wife was curious about a sign in Arabic: "Air wa Bic," which means "prick and Bic." Who wouldn't be startled? It took a long time before his wife could figure it out. It was an Arabic transliteration of "aerobic." His father has also been confused arriving in Hong Kong. Everywhere was the word "Si Da" that was nowhere to be found in the dictionary. The old man was told that it was the Chinese transliteration of the English "store." Drug Si Da, Department Si Da, Thrift Si Da, Jane Fonda Air wa Bic. World civilization has become homogenous from Beirut to Fragrant Harbor. In his conceited attempt to sing in Arabic, he's sure to create similar monstrosities. Still he likes to sing.

"Why don't they put on Fairuz?" he asks vaguely.

That night, there seemed to be only Lebanese in the roof-garden of the hotel in Limassol. The poolside band played a Fairuz song. He was eating *creme de mais* soup like he had as a child at the Bel Air restaurant in Vũng Tàu. Limassol also looked into the ocean. In front of him, the Coke sign in Greek flashed behind City Hall. Farther away, the white waves in the Mediterranean flickered dimly like short-circuited neon lights. The violinist's trembling mustache accompanied the dolorous strains of "Old Jerusalem." Jerusalem Al Khots. It was his first opportunity to hear this melody. The sad tune meandered through the night. There was also a small lamp on their table, shaped like a candle. His wife recounted:

"In 1967, we were let out of school a month early. I stayed home to paint the lightbulbs blue to prepare for the airplanes at night."

He looked around. At each table in the roof-garden the conversation was restrained and polite. Everyone kept his voice low: too loud and they could hear you in Lebanon. It was only across the water, a ten-hour trip by the slow boat plying the Mediterranean. Once it had been Lebanon of the pine-covered hills, of redwoods on summits of cloud-covered mountains— the Switzerland of the Middle East. But Lebanon had turned into pillars of smoke choking the night sky, and Beirut was no longer a city of blue lightbulbs. That kind of air defense had been more romantic than the present system of using SAM missiles. He never heard of children staying home from school to paint SAM missiles bright pink or lemon yellow. Back then, his wife had painted lightbulbs night-blue, ocean-blue, and Prussian blue. At Beirut's Khalde airport, the motley alliance of Palestinians and Lebanese Nationalist troops were holding out against Israeli paratroopers and the elite Golani armored brigade. The evening news announced that the Israelis had cut off the International Highway at Dar El Baidar. Syria's slow-footed 85th brigade was stuck in the city. In the roof-garden, he heard no conversation about the war. The Greek/Cypriot band only grieved over the Allenby bridge. He chuckled: "I've just found that pre-war atmosphere."

Perhaps this special commodity is also available in Orange County. One does not have to take refuge in a roof-garden of a beachside hotel in Cyprus in order to find it. A popular item, he sees it advertised everywhere. The pre-war atmosphere has no definite time span. The Lebanese civil war officially began in April 1975, after a busload of Palestinians got shot up on the unlucky 13th in Ain El Remaneh. To his wife, the pre-war era was before she had to paint lightbulbs blue.

"First Thursday of each month, I would go to my maternal grandmother's to listen to Radio Cairo. The whole Arab world would tune in to Radio Cairo on the first Thursday of each month to hear Oum Koulsoum's new song."

He doesn't like Oum Koulsoum. He has never responded to this ancient, robust woman in black-framed glasses with a kerchief in her hand. On the stage at Gondole, four guys in bow ties are cautiously launching into a melody. It must be one by the musical goddess. The French cultural minister, Jack Lang, in talking about her, had said: "Her voice is a thousand years old or more." He has never liked Jack Lang. But he does like his wife.

"People would smoke hashish, everyone got high—an idle lot. But the only time there was such a thing as an 'Arab Nation' was when a new song by Oum Koulsoum played on the first Thursday of every month."

He looks at the four mustachioed guys in the band and tries to envision Oum Koulsoum, the mythical lover of Gamal Abdel Nasser. Hero of Suez Canal, a thousand-year-old voice, a unified Arab Nation from Riyadh to Tunis, from Baghdad to Tripoli. First Thursday of every month they all fidget with the dial to catch Radio Cairo. Yes, an idle lot—what's so terrifying about them? When Oum Koulsoum went to Libya to perform, young soldiers loyal to Ghaddafi and Jalloud had to postpone the coup against King Idris to go hear her sing. He is no fan of Ghaddafi.

"I went to Damas as a little kid. At the border, there was a large gate with the sign 'One Arab Nation Forever.' I asked my father, 'What do they mean by that?' But he said to ignore it: 'It means nothing.' To me, 'One Arab Nation' existed because of Oum Koulsoum, Abdel Wahab, and Abdel Halim Hafez."

When Abdel Halim Hafez died in middle age, many people committed suicide to be with him. One Arab Nation. He finishes his share of the Mateus and stares at the band with a slight buzz. To him, the pre-war era was before Zouheir Mohsen's death. It has nothing to do with the Egyptian Elvis

Presley, Abdel Halim Hafez. "$15 minimum after 10 o'clock," the little sign on the table reminds him. It's worth it.

The news hit the city at night. The next day, he got his first look at the man's face. Photographs of Zouheir Mohsen at sixteen, Zouheir Mohsen with wife and children, Zouheir Mohsen with Palestinian, Lebanese and Arab leaders. Zouheir Mohsen surrounded by his armed troops. Zouheir Mohsen and Zouheir Mohsen, in French and Arabic newspapers, on wall posters and handout flyers. The name came in short bursts, snatched from harried street corner conversations. Zouheir Mohsen.

"What's happening," He asked.

"Zouheir Mohsen was just killed."

His wife translated perfunctorily, with a worried look on her face. People scattered; at beachside cafés, patrons got up to leave; a few took out their pocket radios. Crowds gathered, dispersed. He tailed his wife, who wasn't his wife yet, only a girl who took him to Rauche to eat roasted corn. In the temporarily peaceful city, Zouheir Mohsen had just been killed.

"Who's Zouheir Mohsen?"

"Leader of Saika. The bastard!" His wife was angry.

Saika was a military organization of the PLO, but controlled by Syria. Since the occupation of Lebanon by Syrian troops, Saika had become the most powerful fighting force.

"Who killed him?" he also wanted to know.

His question had no answer. In that place, there could be no definite culprit. The enemy—Israel, factions within the PLO, subordinates within Saika or Big Brother Syria are all possibilities. Not to mention those with personal motives: a rival in love; an impatient lender; a debtor with no place to hide; a wife or a mistress. Or maybe those with no motives, who didn't like how he looked. Later, it was revealed that Zouheir Mohsen was discreetly vacationing with his mistress in France, at Côte d'Azur. Coming home from gambling, he was shot four times by a stranger with a Banco submachine gun.

Couldn't be saved at the hospital. The old vice of gambling. Saika leader hit the jackpot with Czech-made Skorpion bullets, near Scott Fitzgerald's old hotel perhaps. The Great Zouheir and Eden Roc—very poetic. He snorted once then rolled his eyes, fat oozing from the bullet holes on his bloated torso; his temporary Zelda was wailing like an Arab widow; the French doctor folded the stethoscope and shook his head. As to who the assassin was, even Hercule Poirot would just have to stroke his beard and smile.

His wife didn't need to know who killed him. She only knew there was trouble ahead. She discussed the situation curtly with passersby, pondered, then decided:

"We can't go home by car. Let's walk."

He felt superfluous, like a child, clueless about events. At that moment, it wouldn't do to ask dumb questions such as, "Is it far to walk?" His wife wore faded jeans, a gold-threaded shirt and sandals. Her hair was tucked behind her ears, bound with a brass-inlaid comb. Lugging a large rattan bag, she held a pack of Marlboros and a Bic lighter impatiently in her hands, as the sun set on Ramlet Al Baida. With the shimmering sea on one side, they walked toward town. He shuffled behind her and observed her lithe ass. Since it was not yet dark, he could make out the brand on her jeans, "UFO." By car or walking, wherever she went, his lot was to follow.

As they threaded through an alley, gunfire erupted. From in front or behind, near or far, all over the city the guns called to each other. He listened attentively to sharp bursts doors away and to thin echoes from the suburbs. Sometimes the sounds were urgent and climactic; at other times they were mournful, scattered notes, a Beirut blues. He was a confused dancer, stuck on the dance floor without knowing the tune. His wife led hesitantly, out of sync with the beat. They rushed across boulevards and inched along the walls of apartment buildings. The popping sounds were toy-like—shots fired in panic, to intimidate not to kill. Absent were the hums of grenade launchers or the vibrations underfoot of artillery. Machine guns crackled sporadically. Those with machine guns handy swept bullets across the sky or down the block, for the hell of it. Those with only an AK also joined in. Your turn, then mine. The occasion was the assassination of Zouheir Mohsen. Understanding nothing, he followed wherever she led. On wide sidewalks crisscrossing the city, they staggered to the deadly syncopation. Two quick steps, then one slow step. It was fun following her; maybe one day I'll dare to make her my wife, he thought, while observing her measured steps ahead of him.

Turn left, then hang right. Although the street-level shops had their metal screens down, many lights were still on. Children peered from behind doors. Here and there, old men sat on stools in front of their houses. Young men gathered in groups of three, of five. Older people hurried along, as if late for dinner. It would have been a peaceful neighborhood if not for the sound of gunfire, the wrong soundtrack for the scene. Suddenly, at a large intersection, they ran into the musicians.

He was like a child discovering the basement door. In the middle of the unlit street were burning tires and oil drums, set as barricades. His wife stopped abruptly and entered the gate of an apartment complex. On the stoop, a guy in khaki pants and T-shirt sat with his hands on his knees. Behind him, in the shadow, came sounds of footsteps and excited conversations. He surveyed the dim figures walking around, weapons clanging by their sides. His wife traded words with someone. The guy on the stoop stood up, put his hands in his pocket and turned around to reveal a Soviet-made hand grenade strapped to his pants.

"Can't go home this way," his wife said.

"Who are these guys?" he asked.

"Lebanese. They're blocking the road. The Palestinians are leaving their camp tonight."

A figure appeared in the middle of the road, lit by the flickering light of the burning tires. A Heckler and Koch submachine gun, held in one hand, spat out a few compact bursts. His startled wife turned around. He saw no one shooting back. Since the Palestinians had a pretext to leave the camp armed, local bosses had to drag out their underlings to stake claims to their territories. Skirmishes were not likely to happen; the shooting was meant only to establish realms of control—in the same way dogs would piss on a lamp post. Although the ragged band came up with no tunes, it made enough of a racket to declare its presence, enough to create suspense as spent shells plopped on asphalt. His wife grabbed his hand suddenly.

"We have to go around the other way."

Her hand was clammy with sweat. He didn't pull his back or say anything.

"Watch out or you'll get shot," she tugged his hand.

"They're not shooting at me."

"Watch out for stray bullets," she raised her voice.

He let her hold his hand, pulling him along, and said nothing. Zouheir Mohsen had just been killed; war had begun. For him, the war began that night, at that hour, as she pulled his hand. Crisscrossing bullets on the street provided the mood music. Shoot some more! He wanted the way home barricaded by either the Syrian National Socialist Party or the Organization of Lebanese Communists. Only small arms were involved at that point. Later, should artillery be fired—who knows—she might even hug him.

He reaches out to his wife, who is sprawled at the other end of the U-shaped couch. To eat lying down, Roman style, is pretty enjoyable although no one would do it while hugging. At the next table, the two sisters have company: a middle-aged man, probably the older one's boyfriend. The younger one is there for propriety. While the petite women sucked on their soft drinks, the man whispered solemnly, perhaps about the number of rooms in his newly bought house. The restaurant is filled with Arabs, dressed elegantly for their Friday night.

After fourteen years of bloodshed, those who have wandered to Orange County, on the other side of the globe, have come here to rediscover that pre-war atmosphere—when the sign "One Arab Nation Forever" at the border of Lebanon and Syria could confuse a child; before Zouheir Mohsen was assassinated; when a bus filled with Palestinian refugees could pass safely through Ain el Remaneh; and, even before that, when the Jordanian flag fluttered over Old Jerusalem.

Outside the restaurant, it is as dark as if the power has been cut. It's rural here, lest anyone should forget that Orange County is still hick country. He finds his way to the car, quietly surprised that the two of them had managed to finish the bottle. Another cup and he would have been drunk. He is still in a merry mood, not tired, his stomach not tied into knots, his temples not aching.

He praises himself for his moderation. From inside the restaurant, the music wafts out. Abdel Halim Hafez, with a haircut like the Vietnamese pop singer Che Linh and a boxer's nose, striking a haughty, artistic pose on a fuzzy, cheaply printed cassette cover. He remembers one night in Beirut, after two glasses of arak, he went out to his car singing an old French song to himself. Inside the empty restaurant, the polite waiter had praised him for his singing voice. Encouraged, he couldn't stop. It was probably the only time he had received such a compliment. The Lebanese are a kind-hearted and generous people.

"What song was he singing?" he asks his wife.

"That was the first time I heard it. It's not a familiar song."

"You don't know who it was?"

"No," his wife smiles, "the lyrics were 'Back home, even fire is heavenly . . .'"

"How can fire be heavenly?"

"Flame is hell: 'Oh, my homeland, even your hell is heavenly.' "

"Oh."

"You get nostalgic about home?" he asks.

His wife is still smiling:

"It's okay to be nostalgic every once in a while. The Arabs are like children; always thinking they were the best. They'd get together to hear Oum Koulsoum sing and the entire day would be gone. Now they're on the bottom and they can't understand why, so they cry and tear their hair out. Still, it's okay to be nostalgic every once in a while."

It's like drinking wine, a little bit for fun, but not too much to give you a headache. His wife is very tolerant tonight. The past, what's behind, *The Long Goodbye*, memories. Lyrics to an old song, "It's nothing. Time passes. You know. It doesn't matter . . ." It doesn't matter, although he does not sing it. His wife can only be so tolerant. She's not a waiter at a restaurant on Pigeon Beach in Beirut who could put up with his singing voice. Enough of soaking in that pre-war atmosphere. Let's not abuse it. Think about the past enough to amuse yourself, but don't retch over it. Home or exile, that sour vomit smell can't be made fragrant with mood music. He says vaguely to his wife:

"Where can you get a gimlet around here at this hour?"

Translated by Linh Dinh

A FERRY STOP IN THE COUNTRY

Nguyen Minh Chau

*N*hi lay still so his wife could finish combing his hair. He had a very round head, with hair that was still black and not yet dried out. As Lien stood over the plank bed, meticulously running the comb through his hair, Nhi wondered whether *this one* still remembered that the head of shiny, black hair had once earned him a reputation as a Don Juan. Among his co-workers at the office, he was famous for his youthful look.

When she finished combing, Lien helped her husband to sit up, reaching beneath the cabinet for extra pillows to cushion his back.

Outside the window, the almond flowers had thinned out. This type of flower, even as it bloomed, seemed faded. Perhaps the ones still on the branches were more vibrant than usual because summer was almost over. Or maybe not, Nhi idly thought as his wife spoon-fed him. Maybe it was because the weather had changed. The overbearing heat, coupled with a blinding light that hurt one's eyes glaring off the Red River, had retreated without him noticing.

Beyond the rows of almond trees, the early autumn weather gave the Red River a pale red tint and made its surface seem wider. The sky also appeared higher. The rays of morning sunshine were moving slowly across the water to the opposite shore, where an ancient swath of alluvial deposit displayed its colors of ochre mixed with green—all-too-familiar, these colors were like the flesh and exhalation of the rich earth. Nhi had seen every corner of the globe in a lifetime of travel, but he had never been to this nearby patch of land, the opposite bank of the Red River right outside his window.

Nhi lifted an arm with effort to lightly push away the bowl of bean threads Lien was holding in her hand. He then tilted his head back like a child so his son, Tuan, could wipe his mouth, jaw, and cheeks with a terry cloth soaked in warm water.

He did not dare to look at his son's face. He again turned toward the window, and was surprised to see that the almond flowers showed an even richer hue, a deep purple like the color of night.

After his son had taken the plastic tub away, he asked Lien: "Last night, near dawn, did you hear anything?"

Lien pretended she didn't hear her husband's question. Before her eyes, the broken earth appeared, sloping toward the river. Night after night, the currents displaced chunks of earth and dumped them into her sleep.

"What day is this, honey?"

Lien again didn't answer, knowing what was on her husband's mind. She tenderly caressed his shoulders with her bony fingers.

"Don't you worry. No matter what the cost is, me and the children will always take good care of you."

Nhi noticed for the first time a patch on his wife's shirt. "I've brought you nothing but worries . . . but you never say anything."

"Everything's fine . . . as long as you're alive. As long as your face and your voice are always in this house . . ."

Lien continued after a pause:

"You should stick with the therapy, take your medicine. By October, you will certainly be able to walk again."

"Then, by the beginning or middle of November, I'll take a trip to Ho Chi Minh City."

Lien knew her husband was only kidding:

"You probably won't make it to Ho Chi Minh City, but with a cane, you can probably walk around the house a bit. If you make good progress, I can help you walk down the stairs one step . . . If you're strong enough, maybe even two steps."

"No problem . . . By the beginning of October, I'll definitely make it to the bottom of the stairs."

Lien placed a hand on Nhi's back, where patches of hardened skin oozed pus.

"I'll help you lie down, all right?"

"Not yet. If you need to go to the market or do errands, go ahead. When I need to, I'll call the kids."

After a while, Nhi could still hear the noises of his wife cleaning and instructing the children. Lien then poured medicine from an earthen pot into a small porcelain bowl. Nhi could tell by the sound of liquid being poured and by the smell of the herbal concoction wafting into the room. Lien then walked down the stairs. Again: that familiar sound of a lifetime of one woman's feet treading worn out wooden steps.

Nhi waited for Lien to reach the bottom of the stairs before shouting:

"Tuan, Tuan!"

His son, bare-chested, was sitting with his back to the wall at the top of the stairs, reading a translated novel while snapping watercress. Hearing his father's yell, Tuan ran into the room, one hand clutching a thick book folded in half. "You're tired, Father. I'll help you lie down!"

"Not yet . . ." Nhi scrutinized his son for the first time. Tuan was his second child, away for nearly a year studying at a city way down south, and had only gotten back the previous night. Nhi noticed that his son had grown to resemble him more and more.

The father who was about to depart from this world was holding back a confession in his awkward behavior. He stared out the window one more time before asking suddenly:

"Have you ever been to the other side?"

"What side, Father?"

"The other side of the river!"

His son answered indifferently:

"No . . ."

Nhi concentrated all his energy to articulate the last wish of his life:

"Now you can go to the other side of the river for me."

"To do what, Father?"

"To do nothing." Nhi was embarrassed by the strangeness of what he was about to say. "You go to the other side, walk around for a bit, find a place to rest, then come back . . ."

"What an odd thing you're asking me to do, Father."

"Or, how about this," Nhi refused to change his mind, "you take a few *dong* with you, see if people are selling cakes or fruits over there, and buy something for me."

Yielding to his father, his son got dressed reluctantly and put on a wide-brimmed hat to protect his face against the afternoon sun.

Nhi heard the plop-plop of Tuan's rubber sandals on the stairs and gathered his strength together to drag himself across the plank bed. By the time he made it to the edge of the mattress, he thought he had traveled halfway around the world, as he had done two years earlier on an assignment to Latin America. Exhausted and aching, he paused to rest, his only thought that someone should help him lie down.

Nhi heard footsteps on the other side of the wall. Doubled over and breathing with efforts, he called out weakly: "Hue!"

From the next room, a pretty girl appeared, wearing a boy's tank top and tugging a piece of string in her hand. As a neighbor, she was already familiar with this chore. She addressed Nhi respectfully: "Uncle needs to lie down, right?" Nhi responded between gasps: "Yes, yes . . . my niece." The little girl hopped on the bed, nudged Nhi briefly, then jumped down. She ran to the top of the stairs, jerked the string up and down and yelled at the top of her voice: "Van . . . Tam . . . Hung!"

In a moment, not three, but a whole gang of children ran up. "How are you, Uncle?"

"Hello, Uncle Nhi!"

Surrounded by this mob of children, Nhi thought of the comedy of his situation. He was like a newborn infant, obscenely smiling at the world while soaking in its attention.

The children converged upon him, lifted him up carefully and helped him to complete his trip around the world, from the edge of the mattress to its center, a distance of about two feet. They helped him place a hand upon the windowsill, laid a folded blanket beneath his buttocks and stacked a pile of pillows behind his back.

For some reason, all the children's hands stank of pickles this morning. No matter, that only made him love the kids in his building more.

Sitting next to the window, the first object Nhi noticed was a sail billowing up, catching a gust of wind. The ferry made only one trip a day across the Red River. As it was pushed from the opposite bank, its brown sail, bleached nearly white, hid that inaccessible stretch of land.

On this side, a crowd had gathered, waiting to cross. Some were on foot; others on bicycles. Women, back from the market, were squatting to converse or to pick head lice from each other's hair. He scanned the crowd but could find neither a broad-brimmed hat nor a pale blue shirt.

It turned out his son had only made it to the row of almond trees across the street. Still clutching the novel in his armpit, the boy had pushed his way into a crowd playing elephant chess for money on the sidewalk. Nhi had played elephant chess for money on sidewalks his whole life, and was fairly addicted to it. If his son was not careful, he would miss this one trip across the river. Nhi thought sadly of how easy it is to be sidetracked and bogged down in this life. But what was there to attract his son to the other side of the river? Perhaps only he, who had been to faraway places, could appreciate the beauty and richness of a simple ferry stop right across the river, which enthralled even as it filled him with a fierce regret no words can describe.

Nhi suddenly remembered the day of his wedding, when his wife crossed the river from her village. Lien wore a brown tunic with a kerchief wrapped in the crow's-beak style around her head. Since that day, Lien had turned into a town-dweller. Even so, like that sand bank basking on the opposite shore, her soul had retained its age-old stoicism, selfless and resourceful. After years of restless travels, Nhi had finally found a refuge in his family.

The ferry was more than halfway across the river. From his vantage point, he could even see the patches on the sail, which resembled the wing of a bat, stark against the red water.

As he pictured himself in a broad-brimmed hat and pale blue shirt, stepping on the sand bank like an adventurer, someone coughed behind him. Nhi turned around.

Khuyen, the old teacher, leaning on a rattan cane, was standing near the plank bed. It had become a ritual: Each morning, after getting his newspaper, the old teacher would come by to see how Nhi was doing.

"Grandfather," Nhi gestured with his head toward a corner of the mattress, "little Hue has left a key for you."

"You seem better today, Mr. Nhi."

"Well, I feel like yesterday . . ."

The old teacher suddenly became alarmed. He noticed that Nhi's face was unusually red, with his eyes watery, betraying a crazed desire tinged with grief. Nhi's trembling fingers clawed the windowsill. Drawing on all his energy, he pushed his body forward to thrust a bony arm out the window, as if trying desperately to give a signal to someone.

At that moment, the ferry, making its daily trip across, had just plowed its nose into the steep, broken earth on this side of the Red River.

Translated by Linh Dinh

Authors' Biographies

BAO NINH was born in 1952 in Hanoi. His first novel, *The Sorrow of War*, has been translated into English and many other languages. During the Vietnam War, he served in North Vietnam's Glorious 27th Youth Brigade. Of the 500 soldiers who went south, only 10 survived. His works have been published in *Granta*, in the American anthology *The Other Side of Heaven: Post-War Fiction by Vietnamese & American Writers*, and in the French anthology *Terres des Ephemeres*.

LINH DINH is the author of two collections of stories, *Fake House* (Seven Stories Press 2000) and *Blood and Soap* (Seven Stories Press 2004), and two books of poems, *All Around What Empties Out* (Tinfish 2003) and *American Tatts* (Chax 2005). His work has been anthologized in *Best American Poetry 2000* (Scribner 2000), *Best American Poetry 2004* (Scribner 2004) and *Great American Prose Poems from Poe to the Present* (Scribner 2003), among other places. He is also the editor of the anthology, *Three Vietnamese Poets* (Tinfish 2001).

DO KHIEM was born in 1955 in Haiphong. He emigrated to France in 1975 and now lives in Paris. He is the author of the short stories collection, *The Pre-War Atmosphere*, and a volume of poetry, *Things That Piss You Off So Much You Can't Even Talk About Them*. A French translation of one of his stories appeared in *Serpent a Plumes*; the English version appeared in the Prague-based journal *TRAFIKA*. A poem, translated into English, was published in *The Literary Review*. He is the editor of the important poetry journal, *Tho*.

DO PHUOC TIEN was born in 1966 in Da Nang. When his father, an officer in the South Vietnamese Army, was imprisoned at the end of the Vietnam War in 1975, Tien left school to make a living as a mechanic and a transporter of rice in Saigon. He is included in the French anthology *Terres des Ephemeres* and has also been published in *TRAFIKA*.

DUC BAN was born in 1949 in Ha Tinh, where he still lives. He has published six collections of short stories, three novels and a play. Two of his stories, including the one included here, were translated by Linh Dinh and published in *The Literary Review* in 2000.

DUONG THU HUONG was born in 1947 in Thai Binh. During the Vietnam War, she served for seven years in a Communist Youth Brigade and was the first woman combatant/reporter at the front during the war with China in 1979. She is the author of four novels. Two, *Paradise of the Blind* and *Novel Without a Name*, have been translated into English and other languages. In 1991, she was nominated for the French literary prize Femina (foreign category), and in 1992, she was awarded a Hellman-Hammett grant. A leading dissident, she was expelled from the Communist Party in 1989, and her seven-month imprisonment in 1991, after a speech advocating democratic reforms, sparked widespread international protest. Before her books were banned, she was the most popular serious author in Vietnam (*The Other Side of Illusions*, sold 100,000 copies, and *Paradise of the Blind* sold 40,000 copies before authorities yanked it from the shelves).

LE MINH KHUE was born in 1949 in Thanh Hoa. She joined the North Vietnamese Army at age 15 and, from 1969 to 1975, served as a war reporter. A short story writer and novelist, she won the Writers' Association national award for best short stories in 1987. Among her titles are *Little Tragedies, An Afternoon Away From The City, A Girl In A Green Gown*, and *Collected Short Stories*. Her work is available in English in the collection, *The Stars, the Earth, the River: Short Fiction by Le Minh Khue* (Curbstone 1997).

MAI KIM NGOC was born in 1937 in Hue, and came to the United States in 1966. A physician specializing in pulmonary diseases, he published numerous articles in English in medical journals under his real name, Vu Dinh Minh. He co-edits the influential overseas Vietnamese-language journal, *Van Hoc*, and has translated Lu Tsun and Andre Gide into Vietnamese. His titles include *A Private Moment, A Friend of Literature, Boat People*, and *Rose Bud*.

NGUYEN HUY THIEP was born in 1950 in Hanoi, but spent most of his first ten years in the rural areas of northwestern Vietnam. He returned to Hanoi in 1960 and graduated from the Teachers' College in 1970. His 1987 short story, *The Retired General*, generated hundreds of articles, with some heatedly denouncing its author on moral grounds. It also established him as a major force in Vietnamese literature. Pham Thi Hoai remarked that, after *The Retired General*, Vietnamese writers could no longer afford to write like before. His titles include the *Winds Of Hua Tat, The Water Nymph, Nguyen*

Huy Thiep: Works and Criticism, and a 750-page *Collected Works*, which includes a number of plays. His work is available in English in the collections, *The General Retires and Other Stories* (Oxford 1993) and *Crossing the River: Short Fiction by Nguyen Huy Thiep* (Curbstone 2004).

NGUYEN MINH CHAU was born in 1930 in Nghe An. Along with the critic Hoang Ngoc Hien, he was the earliest champion of Doi Moi literature, with "Writing About War," a 1978 essay that had a tremendous influence on writers. He also led by the example of his fiction, which reintroduced normal people in everyday situations. His books include *The River Mouth*, *In the Footstep of a Soldier*, and *Land of Passion*. A colonel in the North Vietnamese Army, he died in 1989 from liver cancer contracted from wartime exposure to chemical defoliants.

NGUYEN THI AM was born in 1961 in Saigon. From 1980 to 1986 she studied law at the University of Bakou in the Soviet Union. The author of two collections of short stories, *The Sound of a Flute from Exile* and *A Beautiful Woman Fights for Her Life,* her work is included in the French anthology *Terres des Ephemeres*. She has also written a novel and a children's book.

PHAM THI HOAI was born in 1961 in Thanh Hoa. She studied library science at the University of Humbolt in the former East Germany, and has translated Kafka, Bretch, Tanizaki and Amado into Vietnamese. Her books include the short story collections, *From Miss Savage To AK*, *Labyrinth*, and a novel, *The Celestial Messenger*, which has been translated into French. She lives in Berlin and is the curator of the influential literary website, talawas.org.

THE GIANG was born in 1958 in Hanoi. He went to Saigon in 1975 and escaped Vietnam by boat in 1980. A contributor to many overseas journals, he has published one collection of short stories, *Man with Tail*. He lives in Werne, Germany, where he runs a restaurant.

TRAN NGOC TUAN was born in 1955 in Southern Vietnam but raised in Hanoi after the death of his father, a Viet Cong fighter. He studied writing at the short-lived Nguyen Du School at the same time as Duong Thu Huong. He also studied in the Soviet Union. Though he has published only a handful of stories, he has many admirers among knowledgeable readers of contemporary Vietnamese fiction. With no fixed address, he now drifts between Germany and the Czech Republic.

TRAN VU was born in 1962 in Saigon, and fled Vietnam by boat in 1978. He spent a year in a refugee camp in the Philippines and was brought to France by the Red Cross. He now lives in Lyons, where he works as a computer programmer. He is the author of two collections of short stories, *The Death Behind The Past* and *The House Behind The Temple Of Literature*, both published in California. His work is available in English in the collection, *Dragon Hunt* (Hyperion 1999).

Translator's Biographies

BAC HOAI TRAN teaches Vietnamese at the University of California, Berkeley. A consultant for the documentary film *Which Way Is East*, he is the author of the textbook, *Anh Ngu Bao Chi: Introductory Vietnamese; Intermediate Vietnamese*. His translations with Dana Sachs have appeared in the anthologies *The Other Side of Heaven* and *Vietnam: A Traveler's Literary Companion*.

NINA McPHERSON was formerly a journalist in Asia. She is the translator, with Phan Huy Duong, of Duong Thu Huong's *Paradise of the Blind* and *Novel Without a Name*, and a collection of Tran Vu's short stories. Her translations have also been published in *Grand Street, Granta* and *TRAFIKA*. She is working on a film based on the life and war experience of Duong Thu Huong.

CUONG NGUYEN is a professor in the Religion and Philosophy Department of George Mason University in Virginia. His translations of The Giang have appeared in *Giao Diem* and *Vietnam Forum*.

NGUYEN NGUYET CAM taught at the Nguyen Du School for Creative Writing in Hanoi. She is the translator of E.B. White's *Trumpet Of The Swan* and *Charlotte's Web* into Vietnamese. Now living in Berkeley, California, her translations of Vietnamese writers have appeared in *Manoa, The Literary Review* and the anthology *The Other Side of Heaven*. She is a co-editor of *Crossing the River: Short Fiction by Nguyen Huy Thiep* (Curbstone 2004), and co-translator of Vu Trong Phung's *Dumb Luck* (University of Michigan Press 2002).

NGUYEN QUI DUC is the editor, with John Balaban, of *Vietnam: A Traveler's Literary Companion* and author of *Where the Ashes Are: The Odyssey of a Vietnamese Family*. A radio producer and writer since 1979, he has worked for the British Broadcast Corporation in London and as a commentator for National Public Radio. His essays have appeared in *Zyzzyza, City Lights Review*, and *Salamander*.

PHAN HUY DUONG has translated numerous contemporary Vietnamese writers into French and English (with Nina McPherson). He is the editor of the French anthology *Terres des Ephemeres* and author of a collection of short stories, written in French, *Un Amour Meteque*. His fiction is included in the anthology *The Other Side of Heaven*.

DANA SACHS is the author of *The House on Dream Street: Memoir of an American Woman in Vietnam* (Algonquin Books 2000). She is also a co-editor of *Crossing the River: Short Fiction by Nguyen Huy Thiep* (Curbstone 2004), and co-translator of *The Stars, the Earth, the River: Short Fiction by Le Minh Khue* (Curbstone 1997), and *Two Cakes Fit for a King: Folktales from Vietnam* (University of Hawaii Press 2003). With Lynne Sachs, she made the award-winning documentary film about Vietnam, *Which Way Is East*.

PETER ZINOMAN teaches Vietnamese history at the University of California, Berkeley. He is a former Resident Director of the Council On International Educational Exchange's Study Center in Hanoi. He is a co-translator of Vu Trong Phung's *Dumb Luck* (University of Michigan Press 2002). Other translations have been published in *Grand Street, Vietnam Generation, Vietnam Forum*, and the anthologies *The Other Side Of Heaven* and *Vietnam: A Traveler's Literary Companion*.

Credits

"Sleeping On Earth" ("Dao Ngu Noi Tran The") by Nguyen Thi Am. Originally published in the journal *Hop Luu*, number 5, June 1992. First published in English in *Grand Street*, number 48, Winter 1994. Published here by permission of the author. Translation copyright 1994 Phan Huy Duong and Nina McPherson.

"A Marker On The Side Of The Boat" ("Khac Dau Man Thuyen") by Bao Ninh. Originally published in the magazine *Tap Chi Van Nghe Quan Doi*, the Tet issue, 1994. Published here in English for the first time by permission of the author. Translation copyright 1996 by Linh Dinh.

"Reflections Of Spring" ("Hoi Quang Cua Mua Xuan") by Duong Thu Huong. Originally published in the collection *Doi Thoai Sau Buc Tuong* (Hanoi: Nha Xuat Ban Tac Pham Moi), 1987. Published here in English for the first time by permission of the author. Translation copyright 1996 by Nguyen Nguyet Cam and Linh Dinh.

"Without A King" ("Khong Co Vua") by Nguyen Huy Thiep. Originally published in the collection *Tuong Ve Huu* (Thanh Pho Ho Chi Minh: Nha Xuat Ban Tre), 1988. Published here in English for the first time by permission of the author. Translation copyright 1996 by Linh Dinh.

"The River's Curse" by Tran Ngoc Tuan. First published in English in *Literary Review*, 2000.

"Scenes From An Alley" ("Ky Su Nhung Manh Doi Trong Ngo") by Le Minh Khue. Originally published in the collection *Truyen Ngan Le Minh Khue* (Hanoi: Nha Xuat Ban Van Hoc), 1994. Published here in English for the first time by permission of the author. Translation copyright 1995 by Bac Hoai Tran and Dana Sachs.

"The Way Station" ("Dao Cua Dan Ngu Cu") by Do Phuoc Tien. Originally published in the journal *Hop Luu*, number 10, April/May 1993. First published in English in *TRAFIKA*, number 3, Summer 1994. Published here by